VOL. 3, NO. 1   **ISSUE #9**

FEATURES

FROM THE CAT'S PERCH, *by Michael Bracken* 2

NEW STORIES

LAST RITES, *by Stacy Woodson* 3
THE JERICHO TRAIN, *by John M. Floyd* 11
CORAL COVE, *by B.A. Paul* 22
THE ALLEY, *by Ann Aptaker* 31
SONNY'S ENCORE, *by Michael Bracken* 35
SWITCH AND BAIT, *by Cynthia Ward* 48
BECOMING ZERO, *by James A. Hearn* 51
THE MURDER OF JONATHAN GREYSTONE, *by Barry Fulton* . . 64
YOU GOTTA BE IN IT! *by Elliott Capon* 77
THE YOU-DON'T-KNOW-THE-HALF-OF-IT-DEARIE BLUES
    by Michael Kurland 84
A FIGHTER BY HIS TRADE, by Graham Powell 110

CLASSIC REPRINT

SMELLING LIKE A ROSE, by Gil Brewer 123

FROM THE CAT'S PERCH

One of the greatest pleasures of being an editor is discovering new writers through the slush pile. Though the stories by Ann Aptaker and James A. Hearn in this issue aren't their first publications, I included Ann's first story, "The Sweetness at the Crummy End of Town," in *Fedora II*, the second in a three-volume anthology series I edited for Betancourt & Co. (an imprint of Wildside Press) in 2003, and I included James's first story, "Trip Among the Bluebonnets," in *The Eyes of Texas: Private Eyes from the Panhandle to the Piney Woods* (Down & Out Books, 2019).

Since her debut, Ann has written several novels and short stories, and has received multiple awards, including both Goldie and Lambda awards. In the brief time since his first short story appeared, James has placed several more in a variety of publications, and I suspect we're witnessing the early stages of a lengthy writing career.

In addition to stories from Ann and James, we also have Barry Fulton's second published short story, and new stories from Elliot Capon, John Floyd, Michael Kurland, B.A. Paul, Graham Powell, Cynthia Ward, Stacy Woodson, and your editor.

Publisher John Betancourt selects the classic reprint each issue, surprising and delighting me with his choices. This issue we have, "Smelling Like a Rose," a classic reprint from Gil Brewer.

Whether the stories published in this issue are by authors at the beginning of their careers, in the middle of their careers, or, in the case of our classic reprint, well past the end of *his* career, each should bring you joy and delight.

—Michael Bracken
Editor, *Black Cat Mystery Magazine*

Staff

PUBLISHER & EXECUTIVE EDITOR
John Gregory Betancourt

EDITOR
Michael Bracken

WILDSIDE PRESS SUBSCRIPTION SERVICES
Carla Coupe

PRODUCTION TEAM
Sam Hogan
Karl Würf

LAST RITES

STACY WOODSON

Fuzz crawled on my teeth, and my mouth tasted like metal. I flicked my tongue and tried to break some of the funk free. *God, I'd give my left nut for a toothbrush.*

I sucked in a breath. The air was thick and hot. Sweat pooled on my forehead, trickled down my cheek, and flopped against my pillow. The air conditioner must still be broken.

Broken, like we were.

"Good morning, Colonel Wilson."

Nurse Lucy—big eyes, empty smile—hovered above me. She smelled like lilacs, the scent suffocating.

"I'm going to sit you up." Lucy fumbled with the buttons on my bed. The motor went *rata-tat-tat*, stalled…and died. Lucy tried again. This time, it wasn't the bed I heard but the *rata-tat-tat* of machine gun fire.

My heart jackhammered. Bullets whistled past me. Smoke. Then heat— that god-awful heat. Pain ripped through my body. I groped for my pistol, but it was gone.

Gone with my legs.

I blinked. The smoke disappeared, and I'm left with bright fluorescent lights and dingy ceiling tiles. The bed shuddered. The motor engaged. And the hospital ward stuttered into view.

Seven beds. One empty. My men—the ones who survived the ambush.

Everyone, except Pritchard.

"Water?" Lucy poked at my mouth with a straw. I took a sip. Water ran down my chin.

She dabbed at me with a tissue like I was an infant. My face flushed.

"Thank you." I managed. The words were muffled, my jaw still wired shut. Lucy just stared at me the way the Iraqis used to when I butchered Arabic.

Two more days.

Doc Taylor had promised. And then my jaw would be free. At least something on my body would work.

Lucy pulled at the stethoscope that hung from her neck, listened to my chest, and made a note in my chart.

"Don't make no-never-mind to me what you do, but the Boss…he's going to want to know." Specialist Dubois, his Cajun accent thicker than oatmeal, gave someone a ration of grief.

I looked past Lucy to see who was his target. Something orange zipped through the air and clocked Dubois in the head.

"Don't start something you can't finish." Dubois wheeled over, scooped up the foam football and chucked it back at Harrington, still in his bed. The ball fell short and bounced off a table.

"Didn't take you for a knife fighter, Dubois," Harrington snickered.

"You know I'm a good shot," Dubois said. "Who do you think saved your sorry ass?"

I waited for Harrington's smart aleck reply. But he stilled. His eyes misted. And the silence that followed was nearly deafening.

"Thanks, man," Harrington finally said, his voice thick. "Thanks for saving my life."

Dubois shook his head, his face tight. "You'd do the same for me."

"Yeah," Harrington sniffled. "Maybe…"

Dubois's eyes narrowed.

Harrington grinned.

"Asshole." Dubois picked up Harrington's football and tucked it into his wheelchair. "You're not getting this back."

I chuckled, the sound came out like a hiss.

"Boss. You're up." Dubois wheeled over to me, but his eyes were on Lucy. "Hey, cher." He called to her like he was at happy hour in a bar, not at a hospital in a wheelchair.

"Lieutenant Jackson." She corrected him, the same way she did every morning. She moved—*bounce, sway, bounce, sway*—to the next patient. And Dubois's head moved—*up, down, up, down*—with her.

I shifted in my bed. "Dubois."

Dubois's eyes stayed on Lucy.

"Dubois!"

His head whipped back, and he flashed a gap-toothed grin. "Morning, boss." Dubois, my driver in another life, was one of the few people who understood what I said.

"Situation Report."

"Beck, Jones, Laney—no change. Chinn is awake—asking for his mama." Dubois snorted. "Chinn has always been a wuss like that. One time back at Fort Bragg…"

"Dubois."

"Sir?"

"Without the commentary."

"Roger." Dubois frowned. "Who'd I forget?"

"Harrington."

"Gets his leg today. Discharge tomorrow."

"Rooms?"

"Folks been saying the hospital renovation will be done next week. They need to get on with it. I'm tired of hearing Beck bust ass in his sleep."

"Dubois."

"Sorry."

"Lieutenant Pritchard?"

The light in Dubois's eyes dimmed. "Body transported to the States today."

My mind went back to the ambush and Pritch's unending screams. My pulse monitor tumbled into a beeping frenzy. I clicked the button on my morphine drip and waited for the drug to soothe me.

"You alright, boss?"

"Yeah." I forced myself to focus.

"Shame about Pritch. He was a good man. Always fair to us enlisted types. Thought he was on the mend. Even Doc Taylor said Pritch was outta here in a few days."

I nodded and tried to fight through the morphine haze.

"Was surprised the other night, when I saw the Padre visit Pritch. He walked right up to Pritch's bed and closed the curtain. You guys are always bagged out. Those damn narcs they give you. Me." He thumbed his chest. "I stay awake. Someone's got a keep an eye on things. I…"

"Dubois."

"Sorry." Dubois cleared his throat. "Anyway, rumor is the same thing happened in the ward next door. Guy was on the mend. Padre paid him a visit. Next day he was deader than a catfish on Fat Tuesday."

Footsteps.

I looked past Dubois. Father Anthony stood behind him. With his slicked hair and gold tooth, Father Anthony looked like a mobster turned priest.

I shook my head and tried to warn Dubois, but he didn't notice. He was too busy riding his Father Death conspiracy wave.

"Boss, the Padre could've done the same thing to Pritch. You get what I'm saying? If I'm right, none of us is safe."

"Morning Father," I finally said.

Dubois froze, his eyes the size of saucers. He eased back in his seat, looked up at Father Anthony, and went slack-jawed. "Better go…," Dubois stammered, "…go check on Chinn." He zipped away.

"Sorry about that, Father."

Father Anthony chuckled. "No worries. Every unit has a Dubois."

* * * *

"Good morning, Colonel Wilson," Lucy sing-songed. Today, she sounded like a Disney princess on helium. I forced my eyes open. The smell hit me. Not Lucy's lilacs. Ammonia's angry stench. Dread gripped my insides.

Please, not another one of my men.

"I'm going to sit you up." Lucy reached for the buttons on my bed.

Today, the motor clicked like an old reel projector. The bed inched along, and I wanted to scream.

Three, two, one…I'm up.

But I can't see. Lucy, in her heart-covered scrubs, blocked my view.

"Move," I said, my voice surprisingly clear.

"Sir, you really need to…"

"Now."

Lucy exhaled sharply, smoothed her scrubs, and walked away.

I should've felt bad about the way I spoke to her. But I didn't. My view of the floor was clear now. I forced myself to look.

Seven beds. *Two* empty.

Harrington's.

The sheets were tight. His nightstand was empty—like he'd never been there.

That can't be right.

Harrington was on the mend. Doc Taylor said he'd be discharged today. My eyes swept the room like a canine looking for a scent. But I couldn't find Harrington.

Maybe he was already discharged. Lucy would know. I hung on to a small glimmer of hope and pressed my call button.

Dubois appeared at my bed. Shoulders slumped. Eyes red. Harrington's football clutched between his hands. "Boss. I got some news." He picked at the foam. A piece broke free. He stopped and studied it. Finally, he looked up and said, "Harrington's gone."

I swallowed. "Gone home gone?"

"Dead. Gone."

"Jesus."

"I was asleep when it happened. Me. Can you believe it? Woke up when they took him away." Dubois wiped his nose with the back of his wrist. "Saw Harrington's face before they covered him. It was in his eyes, boss. Seen that look before, back home during Katrina."

"Sir, you called?" Lucy was back.

I shook my head.

She turned off my call light and straightened my sheet.

"Morning, cher." Dubois sniffled. Lucy handed him a box of tissue. "Thank you, ma'am." Dubois blew his nose. She patted his arm and walked away.

Dubois put the tissue aside and wheeled closer to me. "Harrington didn't just up and die, boss. Something evil happened to him. Found this on the floor next to his bed." Dubois held up his hand. Between his fingers were rosary beads.

* * * *

"Good morning, Colonel Wilson."

My eyes flew open.

Was Father Anthony here last night?

I was upright but couldn't see. Lucy blocked my view.

"You okay, sir?" Lucy asked.

"Fine," I said, my tone clipped.

She turned toward one of my monitors, and the ward was in full view.

Seven beds. *Two empty.*

No change.

My men had survived the night.

Thank god.

I suddenly wondered if Father Anthony was really Father Death or if Dubois's paranoia had become my own.

Doc Taylor appeared by my bed. "Good morning, John."

"Doc."

Lucy yanked the privacy curtain. The fabric squealed along the track, and she disappeared.

"How's the jaw?" Doc asked, his face buried in my chart.

I moved my jaw from side to side. "Little sore. Not bad."

"After the wire is removed, it's normal to have discomfort. Ibuprofen should fix that." He eyed me over his readers. "No more morphine."

I nodded.

He clicked his pen, scribbled something, and flipped the page. "I see Ortho talked to you about prosthesis options. Any questions?"

I looked at the empty space where my legs used to be. *All I had were questions.* I shook my head.

"No reason to keep you here. You can finish your recovery back in the States. There's a transport that leaves tomorrow."

My stomach tightened. "I can't leave my men."

"Everyone has a different timeline, John. They'll join you soon."

"But Doc…"

"Your soldiers are in good hands." Doc eyed me over his readers again. "Now, let's focus on you. Okay?"

I nodded.

"New hospital policy says you must leave with a care plan." He reached above my bed, pulled a sign from the wall, and flipped it forward so I could read it: *Warrior Care Plan: Do you know your RITEs?*

"RITEs?"

"Record review. Instructions for continued care. Treatment follow-up. Expectations."

"What does the 's' stand for?"

He shrugged. "Hell, if I know. It's part of 'expectations,' I guess. You know the military and their acronyms."

I resisted the urge to roll my eyes.

"Your care will continue with a physician back home," Doc Taylor said, returning the sign to the wall. "Lucy will review the other items with you. I initialed your paperwork." He tore off a sheet from a carbon copy form and placed it on a table near my bed. "This paper is all you need to initiate your discharge. I'll give Lucy a copy. If you have questions that she can't answer, let me know." He smiled. "Good luck, John."

"Thanks."

He weaved around the curtain and disappeared.

For the next few minutes, I reviewed the care plan. When I reached the end, at the bottom of the page, Doc Taylor had scribbled his initials—LST and then RITEs with the date.

The curtain fluttered. Father Anthony appeared with his rosary beads and bible. "Lucy sent me," he explained. "She said you needed last rites?"

I frowned. "Last rites?" My eyes went to my discharge papers and then it hit me. Lucy had mistaken *LST RITEs* with last rites. She had misread the new discharge paperwork. There was no Father Death. Father Anthony had visited Harrington the night before he was scheduled for discharge—the night he died—because Lucy, confused, had sent him there.

Oh god.

I laughed. It started as a rumble and then exploded into a roar.

I couldn't wait to tell Dubois the Father Anthony mystery was solved.

"Sorry, Father," I said, as I fought to catch my breath. "I think Lieutenant Jackson is confused. I get transferred tomorrow."

Father Anthony shook his head. "Poor Lucy. She's been troubled, lately. Her fiancé—a soldier—died in this hospital six months ago. Name was Bobby Jackson. Heard of him?"

"Doesn't ring a bell."

"Lucy was on shift at the time, in a different ward—of course. When she got to Bobby, he was already gone. She's never forgiven herself for not being there when he passed."

"I had no idea." I thought about Lucy, her vacant eyes and empty smile. She was broken just like the rest of us.

The curtain around my bed flew open. Dubois's chest heaved up and down like he'd just finished a ten-mile run. "Everything okay here, boss?"

"Father Anthony and I were just finishing up."

"Blessings." Father Anthony nodded at Dubois. He tucked his bible under his arm and walked away.

Dubois waited until Father Anthony's footsteps faded, and then he leaned in and whispered, "Jesus, boss. Saw the Padre close the curtain and thought he was coming for you."

I laughed. "Dubois, do I have a story to tell you…"

* * * *

Lilacs—the smell filled my nose. I opened my eyes. The curtain around my bed was closed. The lights in the bay were low. One of the ceiling lights flickered, popped, died.

Lucy stood next to me—my IV bag in one hand and a syringe in the other. She pushed the plunger, capped the needle, and dropped it into the pocket of her scrubs.

"Is it morning?" I asked. My voice sounded like gravel.

"Not yet," she whispered. "Close your eyes."

The room swayed, and Lucy's face blurred in and out of focus. "Doc said, no more…" *No more what?* I tried to remember. "…morphine." The word tripped from my tongue. I settled deeper into my mattress, exhausted from the effort.

"Hush now. I've got you." Her words were soft, soothing like the sea lapping against the shore. She leaned over and fluffed my pillow. Her necklace swung back and forth like a pendulum. On the end was a charm with a name written in gold thick script:

Bobby.

I wanted to tell her I was sorry her fiancé had died—that the war wasn't fair. But I couldn't seem to push through the haze.

Lucy tucked the charm under her scrubs and sat in a chair next to my bed. Her face was serene, almost angelic.

More lilacs.

Lucy's perfume filled my nose, again. This time, it was strangely comforting. She tugged at the pulse monitor on my finger. The machine beeped, skipped, and beeped back to a steady pace. She held my hand. Her fingers tightened around mine. The monitor was no longer on my finger. It was on hers.

That can't be right.

My eyes were heavy.

Lucy reached into her scrubs, pulled out a set of rosary beads, and draped them over my hand. "Everything is going to be okay. I won't let you die alone."

Die?

My eyes went wide.

Oh god.
I tried to speak but couldn't breathe.
Help.
Help.
Help.
Lucy stroked my hair. "I love you, Bobby."

Stacy Woodson made her crime fiction debut in *Ellery Queen's Mystery Magazine*'s Department of First Stories and won the 2018 Readers Award. Since her debut, she has placed stories in *Mystery Weekly*, *Woman's World*, *Ellery Queen's Mystery Magazine*, and *Mickey Finn: 21st Century Noir* among other anthologies and publications. You can visit her at https://stacywoodson.com/.

THE JERICHO TRAIN

JOHN M. FLOYD

"Are you sure it will stop there?" Paulina asked.

"It'll stop." Victor Connely lowered the binoculars and glanced at his watch. "In about ten minutes."

She held up a hand to shade her eyes from the midmorning sun. The tiny cluster of buildings in the distance looked like dark pebbles on a yellow-gold carpet.

"How do you know?" she said.

"Because I grew up in these parts. It's been stopping at that station for thirty years."

"I grew up here too. But I do not know the train schedules."

Victor didn't reply. He just gave her a look that said *I make it my business to know things.* After all, he had been raised on the twenty-thousand-acre Connely Ranch and had married the daughter of the late copper baron Alex Larrimore. Paulina was born dirt poor and on the other side—both literally and figuratively—of the tracks. It was a difference they both understood but never talked about. He saw her face harden, and he suppressed a smile. Paulina's fiery temper, never far below the surface, was one of the things he liked about her.

But he didn't need an argument right now.

"Calm down," he said. "In ten minutes—nine, actually—my life's going to get a lot better, and yours too."

Their eyes locked. "And what proof do I have?"

"Of what? That our lives are about to improve?"

"That you will marry me afterward, as you have promised."

He spread his hands. "What more proof do you need? What I'm doing today is for you."

"I thought this was about you getting richer."

"You'll be richer too. In a few minutes I'll become the sole owner of Larrimore Mining, and after you and I are married you'll have everything you ever dreamed of."

Which probably wasn't all that lofty a goal, Victor thought. Six months ago, when he'd suggested to his wife Audrey that they hire Paulina Barros for their household staff, Paulina was a day laborer in a bean field north of town. Victor's foreman, Leonard Ellsworth, had spotted her at one of the markets and pointed her out to him, and Victor had wasted no time making his move. Paulina became Victor's live-in mistress on the same day she became his and Audrey's live-in housemaid. Paulina was young and gorgeous and sultry and had been a wonderful secret companion to Victor these past few months, but—unlike his wife—she was dumb as a fencepost. Victor figured he'd soon be planning how to get rid of her too, and long before he fulfilled his promise to make her the second Mrs. Victor Connely. Right now, though, he had to keep his mind on Audrey. Getting rid of *her* was what they had come here for, today.

Paulina grunted a curse in Spanish. Awakening from his thoughts, Victor looked over to see her trying to adjust the straps of her backpack.

"I do not see why we have to wear these things," she said.

"Because they're a disguise, that's why. I doubt anybody'll see us here, but if they do, we'll look like hikers." Besides, his own pack contained extra water in case they had any trouble with the truck. The bottles were heavy, yes, but he didn't want to be stranded out here in the middle of nowhere and die of thirst. He'd loaded all his gear the night before, as he always did, whether it involved backpacks, suitcases, briefcases, or what, and then put it out of his mind. Victor had never been a Boy Scout, in either name or actions, but he believed in being prepared well beforehand. He added, "This won't take long, anyway."

That seemed to satisfy her, at least for the moment. But as he raised his glasses again she said, in that flat, bored accent of hers, "Did you not tell me you own some of this land?"

"My wife's company does," he said. "Just east of here."

"Then maybe you can answer this." She nodded toward the station. "The railroad line goes all the way to Tucson. Why do they call it the Jericho train?"

"Jericho was a mining camp, not far from here. A booming place, according to Ellsworth. The first rails they laid went only from town to there, and back. I guess the name stuck." Victor squinted again through the binoculars. "Nothing good happens here now, that's for sure. It's just desert. Rocks and dirt. And Tucson's not much better."

Paulina gave him a dark look. "My parents live in Tucson."

"I didn't know that."

"There are many things you do not know, Victor. About me, my family, my past—"

"The past doesn't matter. I'm interested in the future. Yours and mine." He grinned at her and said, "A future without Audrey."

They both fell silent then, watching and waiting. Five minutes to go. The wind whistled and moaned. Ten feet away on the ridgetop, a spotted lizard scurried beneath a rock.

Victor listened hard for the first sounds of the train, approaching from the mountains to the west. Mountains he and Paulina had driven through in his truck two hours ago, while Leonard Ellsworth headed into town in the Lexus to drop Audrey and her luggage off at the main train station. Audrey's plan, suggested by Victor several days back, was to visit her cousin in Tucson for a week. Victor's plan for her was a bit different. When Victor told his foreman about the role he'd be playing in all this stealth and deception, Ellsworth had smiled and replied, *I'm secretive by nature.*

"I still do not understand," Paulina grumbled, "how this is supposed to work."

Victor turned to study her profile. She was staring at the faraway buildings, hands on her hips, long black hair rippling in the dry wind, her own pair of binoculars hanging forgotten from her neck. She seemed completely unaware of her beauty, which to Victor made her even more appealing.

"Then you weren't listening when I told you," he said. "Two nights ago Ellsworth drove to the station there"—he pointed into the distance—"and planted an explosive device at the spot where the passenger car'll be, during the stop. It's hidden in a little opening underneath the rails, on this side of the tracks. While the train's taking on new travelers bound for Tucson—nobody ever gets *off* at Jericho Crossing, just *on*—I'll take out the remote, aim it like I'm about to change a channel on my TV, and push a red button. And BOOM, that's the end of Audrey, the train, the station, and everything else within fifty yards. The blast'll be big enough to see from five miles away, and the smoke from ten times that. Except that you and I'll probably be the only ones to see it, because all around us is nothing but mountains and desert."

He saw her brows knit together in thought. "Fifty yards?" she said.

"So I'm told. Ellsworth knows his explosives. He used to work for Audrey's father, in the mines. He said the MSD for this device—Minimum Safe Distance—is two hundred yards."

"And you are sure it can be done from here?"

"Triggering it, you mean? Yes. Remember what I told you, about our location? Doesn't matter how far away we are, as long as there's a clear line-of-sight. Modern technology."

"If it is so modern," she said, "why could you not push the button while we sit at home, or in the truck?"

Victor closed his eyes. She really could be irritating, at times. "It's line of sight, Paulina. That's the way it works."

"What if somebody parks a car between us and the…"

"Bomb?"

"Yes. Between us and it."

He shook his head. "They won't. No vehicles allowed on this side of the tracks."

"What if somebody happens to be standing there? In the way."

"Then I'll wait till he moves. Don't worry." He patted the right-hand pocket of his vest. "Ellsworth placed the device so I'll have a clear shot at it from here."

"What if the wind blows sand over it?"

"It won't, there in the railyard. And even at great distances, the beam from this thing—think of it as a beam—wouldn't be bothered by a layer of sand. Only thing that can stop it are rocks, or steel, or a brick wall." He paused and said, "Just relax."

Paulina went quiet then. Victor thought he could hear it now: a faint but steady rumble, miles away. The train was still hidden by rolling hills and spiky gray peaks. High above, he saw a hawk riding the thermals, and the straight white contrail of a jet heading east to west.

"What I really do not understand," she said, without looking at him, "is why all those other people must die."

He snorted. "You're getting softhearted, now? I seem to recall you shooting a stray dog last month because he peed on your flowers."

"He will not pee on any more flowers. But these are not dogs we are talking about."

Victor sighed and answered, "This is the only safe way to do it. Audrey'll be one person in a crowd, one of many." He thought, but didn't say, *A lot of them'll be Mexicans anyway.*

"But afterward, the Law will certainly find, how do you say…"

"Evidence?" he said.

"Yes. Evidence of an explosion."

He shrugged. "Doesn't matter. Terrorism's everywhere, these days. And Ellsworth planted the bomb late at night, when nobody was around. No cameras, no witnesses. And there'll be no markings to find, afterward. Nothing to tie the device back to him, or to me."

Silence. Then: "Can you be sure this explosive is in place? At this moment?"

"Yes, I'm sure."

"Because Mr. Ellsworth told you it is there?"

"Yep. He's been with my family twenty years. I trust him."

"And where is this remote thing? This remote that will cause the explosion?"

"It's right here." He touched his pocket again, felt the hard outline of the little cylinder he'd buttoned inside the pocket late last night.

"Show it to me," she said.

"Why?" He picked up the glasses again, scanned the barren flats at the foot of the mountains. The train would appear any second now. Overhead, the hawk was gone, and the track of the jet had faded to feathery white streaks against the blue sky. "Why do you want to see it?"

She hesitated, obviously deep in thought. Finally she said, with narrowed eyes, "Because I am worried. Who else could know about this?"

"What? No one. Just you and Ellsworth."

"I do not mean who have you told, Victor. I mean who else could know?"

"Nobody," he said again. "I don't see what you're—"

"I know when and where you told *me*," she said. "But when and where did you tell Mr. Ellsworth?"

He frowned. "At home, downstairs in my den. The other night, after I left your room."

"You talked about the station, and the explosive, and how and where he would place it?"

"All of that. Why?"

"I will tell you why. What if Audrey overheard you? What if she heard everything?"

Victor blinked. *What?*

"Sometimes you are not as smart as you think you are. Audrey was also downstairs during this meeting between you and Mr. Ellsworth three nights ago. Did you know that?"

"No." Victor and his wife had separate bedrooms, and rarely saw each other at night. Hell, they rarely saw each other at all, which was fine with Victor. Probably with Audrey too; he had long suspected she was having an affair of her own.

"Even more important," Paulina said, "she was gone for three hours last night."

That got his attention. "What time last night?" He'd been at his office until after eleven.

"She left around seven o'clock. In the Lexus."

"And?"

"And I watched her from my window," Paulina said. "Before she left, she put something in the trunk, something long, wrapped in a cloth. But one end of the wrapping fell loose, while she was loading it."

He stayed quiet, waiting.

"It was a shovel."

Victor stared at her. A *shovel?*

"I thought nothing of it, at the time," Paulina said. "Audrey and her country-club friends sometimes do garden things, so this could be—how do you say?—understandable. But at night? And hidden from sight? Now, the more I think about it…"

Victor swallowed. He felt a chill shimmy down his spine. He heard a distant whistle, and was dimly aware that the train had now steamed into view and was pounding east toward the station. Digging out the device wouldn't require a shovel—but would Audrey know that?

"Are you saying—"

"Show me the remote thing," she said again.

He let the binoculars dangle from their strap and used both hands to unbutton his vest pocket. Then he reached inside, took out the remote—

And felt his mouth go dry. A folded sheet of paper was wrapped tight around the cylinder, and secured with a rubber band. Heart hammering, he stripped off the paper.

The cylindrical object wasn't the remote. It was a tiny, cheap, triple-A-battery flashlight. Frantically Victor searched every pocket in his vest. The remote was gone.

Paulina was watching him with wide eyes. When their gazes met she pointed and said, "What is that?"

He looked down at the paper in his other hand, and unfolded it. "A note," he mumbled.

"What does it say?"

On the page was a typewritten message:

SURPRISE, SURPRISE. BOMB IS IN YOUR BACKPAK. DO NOT REMOVE IT—THE STRAPS HAVE PRESSURE TRIGGERS UNDER-NEATH.

He stared in disbelief. After a moment he read it a second time, aloud so Paulina could hear it. His voice cracked; cold sweat trickled down his neck and into his collar.

"Pressure triggers?" she asked. For once, she didn't look bored. She looked stunned. Victor cleared his throat, and tried to clear his mind. "Like a land mine, I guess. Press to activate, release to detonate."

He forced himself to take a long breath. Carefully, his fingers shaking, he reached behind him to feel his pack, and traced the main compartment's zipper to its starting point. Then he froze. The tab had been twisted off and the zipper broken, probably with pliers. It wouldn't open.

Sweet Mother Mary.

Paulina was still watching him. She murmured, "Could Audrey have done this?"

Victor nodded. "She must've. You two are the only ones with access to my closet. I know I put the remote in my pocket and buttoned it—"

"No, I mean *could* she? Does she know about things like…explosives?"

"Oh yeah. She's smart, like her dad was." He swallowed. "Mechanical engineer."

Dazedly Victor turned and glanced south. The Jericho train had now pulled into the station and stopped. Then he looked again at Paulina.

He could see that she was thinking the same thing he was. Audrey must've retrieved the planted bomb from the station and—later last night—put it in Victor's backpack alongside the water bottles. Then she'd taken the cylinder from his vest pocket in the closet, substituted the typed note and flashlight, and rigged triggering devices—if released, they would probably emit signals like that of the remote—inside the straps of his pack. But then another thought hit him. If Audrey now had the remote control…and she was on the train…

And since it required line-of-sight…

Good God.

She might be about to press the red button, right now.

Victor took two quick steps sideways and ducked behind a huge boulder at the very top of the ridge. There wasn't much room there, but at least he was shielded from view of the train. If Audrey couldn't see him—or, more accurately, if her remote device couldn't find him and his backpack—he was safe.

But he would have to stay right here, until the train left. He couldn't remove the pack, and the mountain fell away behind them too steeply here to climb down, and his sheltering boulder blocked the rest of the path along the ridgetop. He also couldn't try to make a run for it back along the route they'd used to get here—it was too open and exposed. He could picture Audrey sitting there on the train in a window seat, aiming her remote at the ridgeline where she knew he would be and clicking its button, over and over. Sending out those beams.

Then an idea struck him. "I need to get to the bomb itself, and throw it away. I have to cut open this backpack." He looked up at her. "Do you have a knife?"

Paulina's face had gone pale. "No."

"I do, but it's in my pack." Then he remembered. "There's a hunting knife in the truck. Locked in the glovebox." He could even see his truck from here, a big Toyota Tundra pickup, locked and parked in the dry wash where they'd left it, half a mile away.

"I will fetch the knife," she said. "Give me the keys."

He handed them to her, careful not to venture out from behind the rock.

She said nothing more. Her jaw set, she shrugged out of her backpack, dropped it where she stood, and then turned and sprinted back along the ridgetop the way they had come. The first twenty yards was in full view of the station—but she wasn't the one in danger.

Victor sagged against his boulder, swallowed again, took a long, ragged breath. *How could this have happened?* He knew Audrey was smart, always had been, but for her to have overheard his plans and drive to Jericho Crossing and dig up the bomb Ellsworth had planted and map out this kind of coldhearted revenge… That didn't sound like his quiet, kindly wife.

Secrets on top of secrets.

All of a sudden he remembered his cell phone. Frantically he fished it out of his pants pocket and looked at the coverage indicator: three bars. He punched in Ellsworth's number and slapped the phone to his ear. It rang once, then connected.

Victor didn't wait to hear a voice. "Leonard," he blurted, "I'm in trouble, I need your help. Audrey found out, and—"

The call disconnected.

"Leonard?"

Nothing. Maybe cell reception here wasn't as good as he'd thought. Victor mumbled a curse, which reminded him of Paulina. Sweating, he scanned the rocky path to the west, the one they had climbed to get here. She was probably halfway back to the truck by now—

And then he saw her. She hadn't yet reached the truck. Instead, Paulina was sitting cross-legged on top of a rock the size of a mini-van, several hundred yards away. He raised his binoculars. She was just sitting there, staring calmly at him.

With trembling fingers he keyed a text message:

What are you doing?

He saw her take out her own phone, look at it, and type a response. Only then did he see that she still had her binoculars with her. That seemed odd. She had jettisoned her backpack so she could run faster, but had taken the heavy glasses with her?

His phone dinged. The screen said:

Minimum Safe Distance. This should be far enough.

What?

Victor sneaked a look around the corner of the boulder. The train was still there, idling at the station.

Quickly he texted:

Don't worry. I'll stay put. Go get the knife!!

The little dots were moving. Within seconds he saw Paulina's response:

Do worry. Bomb is not in your backpak. It is in mine.

He blinked and read the message twice. *Backpak?* Then he looked at her bulging pack, lying on the ground ten feet away.

Another ding. The new text said:

And Audrey does not have the remote.

Victor felt the strength drain from his legs. Numbly he lifted the binoculars, focused on Paulina.

She was holding the little cylinder in her left hand, her thumb poised above its red button. With her other hand she had raised her own binoculars to her eyes.

His pulse was pounding. He understood everything now. He should've understood earlier. Audrey hadn't written that note, and hadn't retrieved the bomb from the station. Paulina had. Paulina had put it into her own pack, typed the note—she couldn't spell any better than she could talk—and jammed the zipper of his pack last night so he couldn't open it today, implying that it contained the bomb. Then, because she knew his habit of pre-packing and never checking afterward, Paulina switched the remote in his pocket with the typed note and the flashlight. She had done it all. The lie about pressure triggers in his pack straps, the lie about Audrey's eavesdropping and the car and the shovel—it had all worked.

Victor moaned aloud. He didn't bother typing his question; Paulina could clearly see his face. With his lips he mouthed a single, miserable word: "Why?"

Through his binoculars he saw her put down hers and type a message one-handed. His phone dinged. He looked down and read her answer:

My mother is on that train.

Victor let out a sigh. He was beyond surprise by now. Again he looked up at Paulina.

She smiled, aimed the remote device…

And pushed the button.

* * * *

On the motionless train, Audrey Larrimore Connely gasped and turned in her seat to face the window. Far away to the north, a column of gray smoke was boiling into the clear blue sky. A deep, shuddering BOOM rolled over the desert.

"What was *that*?" she said to the man sitting beside her.

Leonard Ellsworth leaned forward to look past her. He squinted through the window, then resettled himself in his seat. "A prospector, I imagine. Up on the ridge."

One who's just hit paydirt, he said to himself. *And deserves every penny I promised her.*

Audrey sighed. "Probably so. Sorry—I guess I've become more nervous, lately."

What you've become, Ellsworth thought, *is more rich. Even though you don't know it yet.*

Both of them fell silent. A railroad worker strolled past the window, checking his watch. After a long pause she said to Ellsworth, "Who was that on the phone a minute ago? Who called you?"

"Nobody," he said. "Wrong number."

"I'm surprised there's cell service way out here."

"There's a tower just east of us."

She cocked her head and grinned. "I swear, Leonard. Is there nothing you don't know?"

"What I do know is, you're doing the right thing, leaving him. Both of us are."

Audrey nodded. "I agree." A thought seemed to occur to her then, and she turned again to watch the still-rising cloud of smoke. A semicircular gap had appeared on the horizon, as if a giant had taken a bite out of the ridge-line. "We own some of that land. You think Victor knows people are blasting there?"

"Probably," he said. He was only half listening; his mind was on Paulina Barros. Now, with Audrey looking the other way, he allowed himself a smile. Somehow, that crazy Paulina had managed to do it. He'd given her the bomb and the remote and the instructions and by God she'd gotten it done. She'd told him she would. And Victor had thought she was dumb. "We'll check in with her," Ellsworth added. "When we get to Tucson."

"Him, you mean."

"What?"

Audrey turned. "You meant we'll check in with *him*. With Victor."

He nodded. "Yes. That's what I meant. We'll tell him about the prospecting."

She stared at Ellsworth a moment, her eyes twinkling, then snuggled closer to him and eased her hand into his. "But we won't tell him everything. Right?"

He squeezed her hand and smiled again. "I'm secretive by nature," he said.

* * * *

Moments after the train pulled out of Jericho Crossing on its way to Tucson, a dusty Toyota pickup roared out of a dry wash on the other side of a ridge three miles away. Two of the passengers on the train and the driver of the truck, although they were headed in opposite directions, had two things in common. One was that all three of them had been close companions to a man who had died a sudden and violent death ten minutes earlier. The other was that all three were on their way to new lives.

And if asked, the three of them might've disagreed with a statement recently made by the late Victor Connely.

Sometimes good things did happen, out here in the desert.   ✗

John M. Floyd's work has appeared in more than 300 different publications, including *Alfred Hitchcock's Mystery Magazine, Ellery Queen's Mystery Magazine, Strand Magazine, The Saturday Evening Post*, and three editions of *The Best American Mystery Stories*. John is also an Edgar nominee, a four-time Derringer Award winner, the 2018 recipient of the Edward D. Hoch Memorial Golden Derringer Award for lifetime achievement, and the author of nine books.

CORAL COVE
B.A. PAUL

Peter Shirkey slid the paintbrush, heavy with school bus-yellow pigment, across the final board with one hand and wiped a bead of sweat forming at his shag of a surfer-blond mop. He stood back to admire his effort, his sandals scratching the rogue grains of pristine white sand against the concrete floor. He'd spent a couple of hours this afternoon constructing the mirror-image wooden barricades in the shelter of the one-car garage. The breezy mist threatened to dampen his project, but he managed to scoot the barricades toward the back of the garage. Near his collections.

He couldn't believe he hadn't thought of this before.

The barricades.

How simple. How useful.

He paused the brush over a knot in the wood, a knot about the size of a silver dollar, letting the paint drip into the indentation and coat the dark grain, then gave the entire board one more coat. He'd chosen the least wavy boards from his collection of scrap from behind his uncle's ocean-side bungalow. Well, oceanside wasn't quite right. More like three-blocks-from-the-oceanside.

Uncle's wasn't quite right, either. It belonged to him now.

Peter Shirkey, the handyman, fix-it-guy, jack-of-most-trades for the Bungalows of Briny Breeze.

At least that's what others thought him to be.

And he was good with his hands. He looked at his now, flecked with the bright yellow paint and a dab of white from a touch-up job he'd completed for another home. Gunk under the nails, epoxy and sand and wood putty. A collection of callouses in all the right places, natural protectants from screwdriver handles, wooden hammers, and plastic paintbrushes. And from the tools and motions his own woodcarving hobby required.

He liked his hands despite their use. Strong. Sturdy. Straight fingers and stable wrists filled with muscle memory of all manner of repair work. He'd try to wash up, though, before delivering the barricades.

He aimed two box fans toward the creation and eyed his drying construction. Triangles on one end and simple, single boards angling down from the tips. Just like the street department's, minus the black Briny Breeze lettering across the wood. He'd leave that off. These were his. Not theirs. And he'd need his truck to transport them. Slinging them over his shoulder wouldn't work quite so well.

He returned the paintbrush to the rim of the gallon container setting on the drop-cloth stained with all manner of colors from the dozen or so bungalows his employer owned up and down the shoreline of Briny Breeze. The homes' exteriors were all different shades, marine blue, porpoise slate, peach cobbler, and so on. This helped the vacationers spot their home-away-from-home more easily, and it also helped name the houses. The interiors all had the same two paint colors—sandalwood beige walls and paper-white trim, a suggestion by Peter to his employer. Keep things simple. Keep things affordable. Bank more profit from each booking.

Mr. Williams, the rental mogul of Briny Breeze, agreed. Mr. Williams enjoyed most of Peter's ideas along with his work ethic, and that's how Peter Shirkey at the ripe old age of sixteen had landed and kept his handyman job all these years.

His good ideas along with his collection of scrap and tools helped make the Bungalows of Briny Breeze the success that it was.

Peter had expressed the paint color idea mostly to keep the collection of paint cans from overtaking the entire garage. His pickup, though rarely driven, had to live in the driveway. He preferred to lug his tools of the trade in a canvas messenger bag slung over his shoulder and walk the few blocks to whichever rental paged him.

The school-bus-yellow paint was his own out-of-pocket purchase for the Coral Cove rental, the pinkish-orange house that'd called him this morning about a leaking toilet. And upon his timely arrival the renters complained about the usual—that when they'd Googled this home, the map showed it was oceanside. Which it wasn't. A relatively quiet road and a sand dune separated Coral Cove from the flat stretch of beach leading to the clear blue waters that drew people to the Gulf for rest and relaxation.

"And how do you suppose we're gonna get her all the way down there? What a rip off!"

Peter didn't let the middle-aged woman's rant rattle him as she waved an angry hand, complete with smoking cigarette, toward an elderly woman who sat in the recliner. The old woman's gray hair had been pulled back in a sweaty ponytail. She looked as though she needed a haircut long ago. Not to mention a bath from the long drive here—all the way from Illinois according to the agreement. And, according to this old woman's flat affect, she needed some happy pills.

It looked like the old woman and her probable daughter needed lots and lots of happy pills. The middle-ager ranted on. Unhappy about the location. And the inconvenience of the roadway.

Peter fixed the toilet straightaway with the collection of tools he'd brought with him while she raged on. And once he'd completed the repairs, he explained for the dozenth time this season how simple it was to just walk across the road and down the wooden plank steps to the beach.

He remembered to run his hands through his shaggy hair and smile. Peter's smile was straight and bright white like the clouds that floated over the Gulf. He'd made sure of it. It helped in these situations.

The tank top and swim trunks didn't hurt either. He knew what most women found attractive, and it wasn't the deep scar that ran from the top of his right cheekbone to the tip of his ear. His shaggy hair covered some of it. But he made up for the minor deformity in other ways.

The middle-aged woman calmed and puffed on her cigarette. She let her eyes linger on his cheek. Then his biceps. Peter didn't care. He was used to such gawking. And he felt vindicated that there'd be an extra cleaning fee tacked on for the intrusion of nicotine, but he'd let Mr. Williams and the maid service sort that out.

Peter'd continued. He controlled his voice, soft and gravelly. Not accusing. Not huffy like most his age. He pointed out that Google isn't perfect. And that their rental agreement—that they attested to reading and agreeing to online—noted that a minor roadway separated the house from the beach. And there were pictures. Of the road. And the dune.

But people see what they want to see. And they saw the reduced rates and Google's erroneous pin, which placed the house about a foot from the shoreline—only a touron would believe a house could survive a foot from the shoreline.

Peter Shirkey was only twenty-two, but he knew to not call the clientele "tourons." At least not to their faces. And certainly not in front of such a fine specimen as the third woman he'd seen in the rental that morning.

A gorgeous one. Long, slender hands. Not manicured at all, which was good because Peter didn't like that fake flashy nail treatment. He liked the real nails. This girl's were short. Not bitten down from anxiety like lots of girls through there had. But trimmed. Short. Clean. Her wrists were dainty, but she lugged a suitcase behind her with no trouble and placed it next to the recliner and the ancient woman.

"Granny, what would you like to wear this evening?" The brunette with sea-glass eyes, green and full, looked up with such love at the old woman.

Peter had tried hard not to stare.

"She ain't gotta wear nothin' else. 'Cause she can't maneuver that road and those steps."

"Mom." The brunette rose from her knees. "For god's sake take that outside. The rules. You're gonna get extra fees."

The mother blew smoke directly into the girl's face. "Waste-of-time trip. None of us will have any fun. Stuck here with her."

Peter stepped outside of his garage under the slightly overcast sky and crossed his arms over his chest and breathed deeply to clear his sinuses of paint fumes. The mist had cleared, but the air still hung to the humidity. The ocean breeze would whisk it away. Not too hot this time of year, the end of season when most tourists had settled into their fall routines of school and job ruts. The winter would slow things down further, save for that stretch between Christmas and New Year, and Peter would have time to focus on his collections. And his carvings.

He thought back to that interaction with the family in the Coral house this morning. Thought about how many other interactions like that he'd seen. Four or five that were bad like this morning. Travel and road trips bring out the stress between family and the stupid between friends. He'd seen it season after season.

Three types of people make their way to Briny Breeze. Partiers who were displaced from the north and south cities because the hotels and condos were full-up. They were the cruelest to Peter. Staring. Demanding. Flirting. Some brave enough to try to trace his scar with come-hither fingers.

There were families on fun-filled vacations with whiny toddlers prone to sunburn and mothers prone to spending too much at the neighboring city's mall and teenage girls who didn't quite have the hang of flirting down, but it didn't stop them from trying. Some of those girls would break things in the bungalows just so Peter would have to return. Again and again.

Then there were the kind like at Coral Cove. Peter'd gotten good at spotting these situations. They were the most intriguing. Those families—and sometimes friends—who were fulfilling the last wishes of someone they cared for. A dying relative or loved one who wanted one last dip in the ocean. To hear the roar of the waves before they passed. Warm sand between their toes before their bodies became one with the earth…

He thought about how the mother had stared at his scar. He reached his fingers up and traced it. He'd have to check the mirror before he left with the barricades to be sure he didn't deposit paint into the groove. With each passing year, the blow his uncle had dealt him shallowed and lightened. But it would never be gone. Not all the way.

He turned and faced the open garage. His little bungalow, inherited after his uncle passed, served him well. Simple, white. Not like Mr. Williams's rentals. Peter needed clean and easy. And he hadn't named this place with a corny beach trope either. It was just home.

He eyed the tidy line of tools mounted in neat rows above the workbench. One of his prized collections. Some of those had belonged to his uncle. Some he'd added season after season with his own money. One quality tool at a time.

The long, adjustable pipe wrench with its red plastic-covered handle took high center stage. Mounted above the others closest to the long hanging fluorescent lamp. He felt his scar again. A groove that was once the width of the head of that wrench.

The wrench Uncle had wielded in his hairy ape of a hand when sixteen-year-old Peter had failed to tighten the garbage disposal drainpipe properly.

The wrench that Peter's uncle never used again, and that Peter never touched again after that day—save to hang it here in the garage. As a reminder of how to properly tighten garbage disposal drainpipes.

And to serve as the start of a grand collection of tools.

Peter tapped the top of a yellow barricade. Tacky, but drying nicely. He turned the fan speeds up another notch and fished his keys from his swim trunks. He faced his other prized passion, a steel cabinet running the length of half the garage. He inserted the silver key into the padlock and it gave with a satisfying click.

He slid the doors open. Heavy doors, leveled and balanced just right on sturdy metal tracks above his head swung open like a sliding barn door. Sixteen shelves faced him. Four columns of four. On the first column were specialty tools, rarely needed but prized nonetheless. Stud finder. Electronic level. Ratchet sets in odd measurements. The second column held leather pouches, wound and bound with tie strings. These were filled with wood-carving tools. Whittles. Chisels. Gouges and knives with all shapes of blades, sharp enough to split the hairs on your head. Peter knew because after he finished sharpening them, he'd tug out a couple of his strands and split them. Clean. Simple.

Sharp.

The third column, top shelf, housed his blanks, the size of his hand in all directions. A little taller than wide. Basswood in the palest shades, soft and easy to handle. Mahogany for deeper hues. A few blanks of walnut.

The fourth column held the start of his most prized collection. Five hand-sized basswood blocks hollowed out, filled with a memento, then corked with tupelo and sealed with epoxy. On the outsides, he'd etched and carved reliefs honoring the people he'd met. A loved one. Acquaintances. Strangers filled with kindness toward him.

He ran his fingers over the blocks. He chose his first piece, made in honor of his uncle despite the man's hostility, and took it from the shelf. Peter had captured his uncle's ape hand perfectly. Knobby knuckles. Protruding veins of old age. Even the darkening liver spots. He'd needed a photo to work from of course, and the family album hadn't failed him.

He'd found photos of his uncle at work, holding the tools of the trade. Holding the red-handled wrench. Holding beer cans. Holding Peter as a baby.

After Peter had practiced on spare pieces with various tools and stains to match the image just right, he'd burned all those photos and just kept this one remembrance. He shook the box. He could hear the old wedding ring bobbing around inside, bumping against the basswood.

Peter replaced the carved memorial back on the shelf and admired the other four. Four who suffer no more. One final sunset. One final dip in the ocean.

After his visit to Coral Cove this morning and all while assembling and painting the barricades, Peter thought of this shelf. Of hollowing out another blank. Of carving another relief onto its front. Dreaming of capturing the hands he'd seen there.

He thought of those sea-glass eyes. The way they didn't linger as her mother's had on his scar, but they'd seen *him*. And only him.

And when he'd pulled the girl aside—Ellen, she said her name was—to tell her of his plan, her face lit up, freckles smattered across her nose and lips turned up into a perfect crimson arch. She'd covered her mouth in gratitude and her eyes had teared up. Covered her mouth with those perfect hands.

Peter shuddered. Maybe from the anticipation.

Maybe from the box fans.

He slid the doors to his steel cabinet closed and clicked the padlock shut. He dropped the keys back into the pocket of his trunks and unplugged the fans. The paint was dry. Finally. He hoisted the wooden barricades one at a time over his shoulder and loaded them carefully into the back of his pickup.

Peter closed the garage door on his meticulous collections and headed for Coral Cove, barricades rattling in the back of the truck. Windows down, hair blowing in the briny breeze. A perfect evening to help an old lady with her last wish.

The walk to Coral Cove this morning had taken five minutes. The drive is shorter. Up the road about two miles is the hot spot with towering hotels and condominiums. The high-rent, hot-party district. Down the road about the same distance is another hot spot, similar hotels and condos. Briny Breeze was a tiny burb of both of the hubs, and mostly, especially this time of year, traffic didn't flow too heavily or too quickly.

But the Coral Cove family insisted that old granny couldn't make it across the road without a meltdown. And they feared she'd be too fearful of crossing at all if there was traffic. Peter stopped the pickup at the first T in the road before Coral Cove and dropped a barricade in the middle of the street. He drove the other barricade to the next T and set it in the street, forcing any vehicles to take a simple, clean, one-block detour behind the bungalow.

He knocked on the patio door. Ellen answered, all crimson smile and freckles. She held out her hand to him. His heart fluttered. He took it and tried not to stare at her fingers or her eyes. "I can't believe you're going to help with this. This is the whole reason we came. Mom left. It's just us. I told her I'd watch Granny while she went and did her own thing." Ellen rolled her eyes. "Mom always needs her 'me time'."

"I understand." Peter dropped Ellen's hand before it became awkward for the girl. He focused attention on the old lady, still in the recliner. Still with the greasy ponytail. "Hello, ma'am. Are you ready?"

She smiled. A yellow, partly toothless smile.

"Granny doesn't talk much. But she'd told me before the last radiation treatment that this is what she wanted to do before she died. She and Gramps met on a beach like this. I promised her. Spent my own money to get the three of us down here." Ellen took the old woman's hands in hers and caressed her fingers. Brought them to her mouth and kissed them.

Peter cleared his throat and shuffled his feet. "Well, let's do this before someone calls the street department on me." He grinned his bright white smile and mustered all his willpower not to stare at those hands. Either set of them.

Ellen gripped her grandmother's armpits and helped the woman to her feet. After standing for a few seconds, the woman smiled and followed Peter outside. When the women saw the barricades, the grandmother clapped and Ellen covered her mouth with those fingers again. With Peter on one side of Ellen's grandmother and Ellen on the other, they helped her cross the asphalt, over the yellow and white lines and onto the wooden landing atop the dune overlooking the ocean.

And this time the grandmother covered her mouth with both hands and cried crystal-clear tears from those vacant eyes. She nodded at Ellen in appreciation but then pointed to the steps and shook her head.

"Ma'am. If I may." Peter touched the woman gently on her elbow and took one of her hands in his. He could feel the frailty of the years radiating from her fingertips. Her nails needed trimmed, yellow and brittle and striped with calcium deposits. An aged gold wedding band spun loosely on her left fourth finger. He held her hand to his chest and spoke clearly, cleanly into her ear. "Would you like me to carry you?"

The vacant eyes widened and an ornery smile grew across her face.

Peter smiled back. "I'll take that as a yes."

"Piggy-back or bride-style, Granny?" Ellen asked.

The old woman pointed to Peter's back. And grinned again.

Peter dropped to one knee and Ellen helped her grandmother drape her arms around Peter's neck. She hoisted the woman from the back and Peter rose carefully, tucking his hands under the woman's thighs. She probably weighed one-twenty dripping wet. Her long, gray mane tickled Peter's nose as they started down the wooden steps.

He carried the woman, with Ellen steadying as they went, all the way to the water's edge. Ellen commented that life was cruel but how she would always remember Peter for his help. The sun was about two inches from dipping its bottom into the Gulf. Plenty of time for the old lady to enjoy the shore.

One last toe-wetting.

One last sand-stepping.

One last sunset before it all ended for her.

Ellen brushed away tears. Peter set the woman down gently and made sure she was as steady on her feet as she could be. Ellen eased the woman into the shallow ebb and flow of saltwater. Peace filled both of their faces. Peter took several steps away to give them privacy.

And to watch. How they held hands. How Ellen touched the woman's face. How the woman touched Ellen's. How Ellen playfully splashed the old lady. The grins.

The sea-glass eyes.

Those hands.

When the lady'd had enough, Ellen helped her to a sandy ledge and edged her down to a sitting position. The old woman gave a thumbs-up and Ellen joined Peter several feet away. They stood silent, watching gulls swoop and dive. Watching the shallow waves tickle the sand. Watching the old woman enjoy one last sunset in this vast openness.

"It's cruel."

"What's cruel?"

"Death. Age. Watching her deteriorate. I wish…" Ellen stopped herself. She looked up at Peter. Not flinching at his scar. Squared her jaw. A dark shadow crossed her eyes. One that Peter knew well.

He'd been careful to keep his own dark shadows in check.

"You wish what?" His heart beat so hard he thought Ellen would be able to hear it over the gulls and the waves.

"I wish I could…help her. Things are gonna get worse. Mom keeps hauling her to chemo and radiation, bawling and squalling that she doesn't want her to die, but you saw how my mom is. And Granny doesn't want that. I know that. She's suffered enough." Ellen took a step backward and shook her head as if awakening from a dream. "I've said too much. I guess it's because I know I won't see you again…I just—"

"I had an uncle who suffered. I didn't like watching that, either," Peter ventured, taking a tiny step into the deep.

"What did you do?" Ellen crossed her arms over her chest and looked at her grandmother. Then back to Peter. "Did you…help him?"

Peter's mouth went dry. Could this girl be real? These questions? Someone like him? Peter took another step. Knee deep into the deep. He nodded.

Ellen's eyes widened. She took his hand in hers. His heart went from palpitating to retreating into his bowels.

"It's merciful, right?" She looked up at him. Longing for an answer to her problem. Longing for…peace.

He nodded again.

"Help me."

"Really? Are you sure?"

She nodded, tears flowing down her cheeks. He brushed them away and wondered how his callouses felt against her freckles.

To have a partner. Someone to confide in. Someone to help release others from their suffering as he had with his uncle.

As he'd done with four other decrepit ones hauled to the beach and then abandoned by uncaring family to fend for themselves in the bungalows when the treks to the water proved too much. Aged and alone and afraid in Briny Breeze.

They retrieved the old woman, who'd drifted off to sleep watching the sun as it slipped halfway into the water. Peter scooped her up like a child, her head resting on his shoulder, so she could look at the ocean all the way up to the top of the dune. Watch the golden orb disappear completely into the Gulf.

One last sunset.

As they climbed the dune back to Coral Cove, Peter Shirkey imagined his skilled hands guiding Ellen's novice ones over the surface of a basswood blank, helping her capture the lines of her grandmother's digits and wrist.

And he imagined the sound the old woman's yellow wedding ring would make in the hollowed-out basswood box.

Beth Paul started writing epic space sagas using dull #2 pencils on wide-ruled notebook paper in grade school. She's since upgraded her writing implements and has published short stories in *Ellery Queen's Mystery Magazine* and *Pulphouse Fiction Magazine*. Three of her shorts have earned Honorable Mention from L. Ron Hubbard's Writers of the Future Contest. You can find her books, story collections, and free fiction at bapaul.com.

THE ALLEY

ANN APTAKER

Death wasn't what Howard Vickers had in mind for his Saturday night. He'd planned to stop in at his favorite bar down the street from his apartment, enjoy a little drinking, a little dancing, a little conversation and laughter. He even figured he might get lucky and go home with a willing woman, maybe that curvy redhead who dropped by the bar now and then. But Howard never made it to the bar. A shadow waited for him in the street, a shadow that followed him, slithered near him, and finally cornered him. The shadow, when it dissolved in the glare of a streetlight, took the form of a wiry, cold-eyed man in a gray overcoat holding a .45 semi-auto. Howard knew the man with the gun, a man he figured would find him sooner or later. His name was Louie Sharp.

So instead of enjoying a night of liquor and laughter and the warm body of a woman, Howard Vickers took refuge in a cold, dark, damp alley, stalked by death.

Louie was at one end of the alley. Howard was trapped at the other. There was no exit. The alley ended in the back wall of an old movie theater, out of business and converted to a shady church long ago, the kind of place that promises to fill your soul while it empties your wallet. Seeing the name of the church, The Love of God Tabernacle, painted on the back wall, Howard squelched a laugh, a dangerous bleat that could give him away, let Louie catch the sound and find him. But the name of the church struck Howard funny because right now he wouldn't mind handing over a few bucks for The Love of God if its crooked reverend could work a miracle and sneak him past Louie Sharp.

The only places for Howard to hide from his stalker were behind the dumpsters lined up like green sentinels on either side of the alley, or in the shadows made by the dumpsters, big black squares of sepulchral darkness. He crouched behind a dumpster. He could hear Louie's slow, purposeful footsteps tap and scrape along the alley. Howard knew that pretty soon he'd even be able to hear Louie's breathing, and Louie would be able to hear his. Howard knew because Howard Vickers was as much of a killer as Louie Sharp. In the trade, Howard was known as the Merchant of Death because he sold his skills for high prices. Louie was known as the Angel of Death because, like angels, he appeared out of nowhere. You saw him only when he wanted you to.

Howard heard Louie's footsteps coming closer to his hiding place, the footsteps stopping now and then while the Angel of Death searched a shadow or behind a dumpster or poked around inside one. Louie's thoroughness gave Howard time to think, time to work out a possible means of escape. The odds were slim and he was at a disadvantage, being unarmed because he'd planned a night of whiskey and women, not dealing out death or dueling with it. But his finely tuned instincts of a professional killer were in high gear now, nerve ends bristling electric under his skin. He listened for the rhythm of Louie's footsteps. He calculated how long it would take for Louie to arrive at his hiding place. Two minutes, maybe three, as Louie worked his way back and forth along the alley, checking behind and inside the rows of dumpsters.

Howard decided his best bet was to keep moving, slip between shadows and the dumpsters. He'd have to do it quietly. He'd have to be unheard, or Louie's equally finely tuned senses would find him. But if he could slip past Louie and make it out of the alley and back to the street, he stood a chance of escape. He'd get lost again in new crowds on new streets in a new city.

The crinkle of plastic garbage bags signaled to Howard that Louie was searching through a dumpster on the other side of the alley. With Louie thus engaged, Howard made his first move. He sidled, crablike, into a shadow, crouched there while Louie poked around in the bags of trash. Howard then sidled to another dumpster, sliding behind it just in time before Louie came back across the alley.

Howard repeated this process again, and then again and again and again, slowly working his way back toward the street until he was forced to stop. He heard Louie's breathing nearby, heard his thin, wheezy, "I know you're in here, Vickers. You're a dead man. You know you're a dead man." And then Louie said nothing, letting the whisper of his breath slide along the walls and drift into Howard's ears.

Despite the damp chill in the alley, sweat dripped down Howard's face and neck, trickled under his collar and down his chest. The hot, salty sweat stung his clammy flesh. In this standoff between Howard and death, time seemed to slow down, allowing Howard's mind to work like gears in a slowly turning, tightly calibrated machine. He calculated the space between the shadows and the dumpsters, the distance along the alley to the street, the chances of getting the drop on Louie, grabbing his gun and killing him.

But there were unexpected clogs in the gears of Howard's thinking. In the slowdown of time and the darkness of the alley, odd thoughts crept up like wagging fingers plucking things from Howard's mind, waving unwanted pictures of people, of scenes, of deeds best laid to rest: the wife Howard cheated on and swatted around; the men and women he'd gunned down or strangled or knifed; the money he stole from the big shot who hired Louie to come after him.

Fear such as he never felt grabbed hold of Howard, a terror so cold it threatened to freeze his bones. He was afraid that if he moved, his skeleton would shatter like a million shards of ice. He knew that Louie Sharp, the Angel of Death, was relentless in pursuit of prey, and so was the big shot who hired him, the powerful guy with his fingers in every dirty deal, every politician's underwear drawer, every financier's hidden assets. Howard remembered the time, not so long ago, when he'd been Mr. Powerful's chief dropper, hired to get rid of impediments, interlopers, rivals, big mouths or just plain pests. It was a great gig, paid higher than all of Howard's other gigs, brought him to the edge of being a rich man. And that was the trouble. Seeing how the big shots lived, the things they bought, the women they had, Howard wasn't satisfied with being nearly rich. He wanted the prime cut of meat, the filet mignon on a gold plate. So he did a stupid thing, did it over and over until his scam was discovered and now it was Howard who Mr. Powerful had marked for death.

And who was the snitch who'd ratted him out? Louie Sharp. It was Louie who'd stumbled onto Howard's scam of inventing threats to Mr. Powerful, convincing the guy to have each invented perpetrator rubbed out and then bringing back phony evidence of a job well done: a finger or an ear from the corpse of another job; a photo of another body, cut up and unidentifiable. Easiest money Howard ever made for doing absolutely nothing.

But it all crashed when his game was found out, and the crash brought him here, cringing behind a dumpster in a damp alley in another city, a city where he wasn't Howard Vickers, he wasn't the notorious Merchant of Death. He was just a guy with a gun who, for a small, unnoticeable fee would get rid of life's annoyances: the unwanted spouse, the petty boss. The big bucks were behind Howard, but he'd stayed alive, stayed out of the path of Mr. Powerful's vengeance.

Until tonight.

It had to happen. Howard always knew it had to happen. Big shots didn't get to be big shots by being fools or letting things slide. Mr. Powerful would demand retribution. And Howard knew, too, it would be Louie Sharp who Mr. Powerful would hire to come after him. Louie was the obvious choice, because Louie Sharp, the Angel of Death, was the only killer for hire as good, as relentless in the pursuit of prey as Howard Vickers.

The cold of the damp wall against Howard's back penetrated his coat and seeped down to his skin. He shivered. The cold seemed to grip him, wrap around him like a coffin.

He wondered, for the first time in his life, what death actually felt like. Was it cold like the alley wall? Did death come with a shriek or was it as quiet as its home in a tomb? He wondered what his victims felt when he killed them. Did terror grip them? What did they see when the bullet or the knife punctured their bodies, or when Howard's hands broke their necks or choked the life out of them? He wondered if things suddenly went black or was there that light that people talked about when they came close to death but didn't go over after all? He wondered if there's a heaven or if there's a hell? Is there a room already reserved for him in hell? Will Satan give him a welcome basket of rotting meat?

He blurted a laugh, he couldn't help it, couldn't squelch it, because it was suddenly all too funny to be trapped in an alley overseen by The Love Of God, stalked by death's angel, while he, Howard Vickers, the infamous Merchant of Death, mulled over his sins and mused about heaven and hell and getting the devil's greeting.

And so he laughed, loud, hearty laughs that Howard knew risked letting Louie Sharp track him even as he continued to sidle through the shadows along the wall of the alley toward the street, toward the freedom of crowds, toward the chance to escape death. He laughed when he heard the scrape of Louie's shoes, laughed when he looked up and saw the silhouette of the Angel of Death, and when he heard the shot he laughed and thought: "Not a bad way to go, to die laughing."

Ann Aptaker's Cantor Gold novels have won the Lambda and Goldie awards. Her short stories have appeared in the *Fedora II* and *III* anthologies, the *Mickey Finn: 21st Century Noir* anthology, *Switchblade* magazine, and the online zine *Punk Soul Poet*. Her novella, *A Taco, A T-Bird, A Beretta and One Furious Night*, is featured in season two of the Guns + Tacos crime fiction series. After a thirty year career as an art curator and exhibition specialist for museums and galleries, she was a professor of art history in New York. In between, Ann did a stint as an investigative report writer for a private investigations firm in Novato, California. Ann now writes full time.

SONNY'S ENCORE
MICHAEL BRACKEN

On a cool Tuesday evening in September 1935, much of the adult population of Granbury, Texas, came out to see Sonny Goodman and His Orchestral All-Stars, paying twenty-five cents a head to watch the seventeen-piece band perform the most popular swing tunes of the day. The band leader, a female vocalist, and a bus driver rounded out the twenty-member traveling troupe, which performed several nights a week throughout the Southwest.

Shortly after midnight, as the musicians gathered their charts, packed their instruments, and broke down their music stands, Sonny presented each of them with their share of that evening's take.

Two dollars.

He kept the rest to cover expenses—fuel for the bus, the printing of handbills, pay for the advance man who preceded them into each town along their tour route, and more.

They had almost finished packing when the second trumpet and the third saxophone—neither of whom had performed that evening—joined them and pressed a wad of currency into Sonny's hand. As he slipped the bills into his pocket, Sonny asked, "How much did you get?"

"We didn't have time to count."

* * * *

Sonny didn't look at the money until everyone was aboard and the bus had left the Granbury dance hall far behind. Then, with only moonlight leaking through the dusty bus windows for illumination, he counted one-hundred-eighty-seven dollars in small bills, more than twice what the band earned performing five hours of swing music.

Wanda McDonald, the redheaded chanteuse who joined the Orchestral All-Stars at the height of the Depression, slid onto the seat next to him. The form-fitting black cocktail dress she wore onstage hung over the window on her side of the bus, and she wore a thin blue robe sashed at the waist that did little to disguise her buxom, wide-hipped figure. Her unpinned hair crashed in waves to her shoulders, and she pushed a stray lock away from her emerald-green eyes as she nodded at the wad of cash in Sonny's hand, "How'd the boys do?"

"We'll be eating steak and sleeping on mattresses tonight."

"It's been a while."

"Too long," Sonny said.

He rested his free hand on Wanda's knee and slid it under the hem of her robe. Before it traveled more than a few inches, she wrapped her slender fingers around his wrist, lifted it from her thigh, and returned his hand to his lap.

"Don't be trying to seduce me with promises of fine things," Wanda said. She had joined on the recommendation of Andy Stewart, their advance man, after the band's previous singer tired of the road and returned home to marry her high school sweetheart. "I won't be able to restrain myself."

Wanda returned to her seat behind the driver on the opposite side of the 1929 Dodge Brothers bus purchased new three months before the stock market crashed, when Sonny was flush with cash after playing month-long gigs at large venues in Chicago, Indianapolis, St. Louis, Kansas City, and other major cities throughout the Midwest. The bus seated forty plus the driver, but the band lived out of the bus and packed it with their instruments, charts, music stands, clothing, and personal items, leaving little room for anyone but Sonny and Wanda to stretch out. The windows, which could be lowered to allow in the cool evening breeze, were closed tight against the dust kicked up by the bus's big wheels, and many of the musicians cooled off by stripping down to their skivvies before trying to sleep. Behind Wanda, the drummer had already fallen into a deep slumber, and his snoring lacked any recognizable rhythm.

Sonny watched the singer shift position several times before finally closing her eyes. Then he leaned forward and asked the driver, "How much longer?"

"If'n the road don't get no better," replied Elmer MacDonald, "I be drivin' all through the night."

* * * *

Sonny Goodman and His Orchestral All-Stars rolled into Chicken Junction just after sunrise Wednesday morning. Elmer parked the tour bus in front of Flo's Diner, and one-by-one the musicians woke, stretched, and made their way inside. They kept Flo and her waitress busy for the next hour serving bacon and eggs and toast and coffee thick as motor oil that a few musicians diluted with generous pours of cheap whiskey from their hip flasks.

Later that morning, Sonny rented eleven hotel rooms at The Potter Hotel in downtown Chicken Junction—a single for himself, a single for Wanda, and doubles for the rest of the troupe. They shared the hotel with oilmen and traveling salesmen but kept mostly to themselves.

After lunch in the hotel dining room, Sonny located the post office three blocks away and collected a package awaiting him at the General Delivery window. Once back in his hotel room, he opened it and spread the contents across his bed next to his open suitcase.

The band's advance man had booked them a Thursday evening gig in Quarryville, a town just down the state highway from Chicken Junction. As was often the case since the beginning of the Depression, the band would earn a percentage of the cover charge, but their earnings from performing were unlikely to be their greatest source of revenue that evening. Included in the package were a hand-drawn map of Quarryville with the location of the dance hall and the granite quarry's business office clearly indicated, and a rather artistic rendering of the office building indicating likely entry points for someone lacking keys. Also included was a note indicating that the quarry paid employees in cash every Friday, that the cash was delivered from the bank late Thursday afternoon, and that it was sorted into pay envelopes before being stored in the safe overnight. He had just finished reading the note when someone rapped on the hotel-room door.

The knock was followed by the singer's voice. "Open up, Sonny. It's Wanda."

Sonny opened the door and let her in. When she saw everything on his bed, her eyes lit up. "What's the score?"

"Payroll office in Quarryville."

As Wanda stepped across the room, he quickly closed his suitcase, hiding his snub-nosed .38 and the cash remaining from previous jobs. She examined everything on the bed as closely as Sonny had. "If Andy's right, this will be our biggest score ever. What's the play?"

"We'll need Bernie for the safe."

Bernie tickled the ivories. Wanda glanced up at Sonny. "He'll be missed."

"Stan can double on piano. He isn't as good as Bernie, but he'll do in a pinch. These rubes won't notice the difference."

"Who else?"

"I'm thinking Carter for the muscle."

Carter played fourth trombone.

"Just the two?"

"We'll put Elmer on lookout."

* * * *

Sonny Goodman and His Orchestral All-Stars never intended to become a traveling band of thieves but supporting themselves as musicians had been a financial roller coaster even before the Depression wreaked havoc with the dance halls and night clubs that hired them. Their first crime had been one of opportunity when the saxophones spent the second intermission smoking reefer in the alley behind a Dallas nightclub three years earlier. Tommy Turner leaned against a door on the far side of the alley and fell backward into a pawn shop when the unlatched door swung open. Not one to overlook opportunity, he spent several minutes poking around while the other saxophones kept watch. By the time they returned to the nightclub stage, they were seventeen dollars richer and the pawn shop's alley door was locked as tight as it should have been earlier.

Within days the rest of the band realized the saxophones were flush with cash—as flush as seventeen dollars split five ways could be—and demanded to know where the money had come from.

Tommy told them what had happened and finished with, "When opportunity opens the door, you walk on through."

"How many other doors might opportunity open if we checked the locks?" Bernie asked.

Several conversations broke out, with musicians on all sides of the issue. Those in favor of eating regularly seemed to be tipping the scale toward income-producing extracurricular activities before Sonny finally reined everyone in.

"We're not about to go all Bonnie and Clyde," he said, "so no guns. If we do this, we need to plan carefully. And whatever we get, we share equally. No solos."

After much discussion, the emptying of several hip flasks, and the smoking of a few reefers, they realized many band members had juvenile records involving shoplifting, pickpocketing, and petty larceny. They also realized that most of those without records had just never been caught. A week later, Sonny brought the advance man up to speed, and soon he was casing potential burglary targets as carefully as he was vetting performance venues.

Within three months, they perfected the use of General Delivery to transmit critical information about potential targets. By then, Sonny better understood the non-musical talents of each of his musicians. He knew which were best for strongarm jobs and which were best for those that required finesse. He also knew the group's musical charts, so he knew how to plan an evening's repertoire to minimize the absence of any musicians.

* * * *

Heist of the quarry payroll would just be one more in a series of crimes that had kept the Orchestral All-Stars swinging along when so many other touring acts had disbanded. Sonny brought in Bernie, Carter, and Elmer and went over the plan multiple times before dinner.

Their greatest concern was the drive from town out Quarry Road, the farthest distance from a dance hall any of the band had ever traveled for their extracurricular activities.

"How we going to get out there?" Carter asked. "We can't take the bus."

"I'll get us a car," Elmer said. "Y'all just be ready to go when I pull up to the back door."

"You'll have three hours," Sonny explained. "We start at eight and wrap things up at eleven."

"Fifteen minutes each way," Elmer said. "Give or take. That's more than two hours inside to open the safe. You good with that, Bernie?"

The piano player cracked his knuckles and reexamined the information from the advance man. "If Andy's right about the make and model of the safe, I should have it open in less than fifteen minutes."

* * * *

The next morning, Sonny Goodman and His Orchestral All-Stars were well rested and well fed, so they were in a jovial mood when they unloaded the bus behind the Quarryville Grange Hall. Though they all knew which musicians would be missing from the stage that evening, none but the involved were privy to the details of the impending burglary. Sonny preferred it that way. The less the musicians knew, the less likely they were to accidentally spill the beans on one another.

They left two music stands on the bus and arranged the other fifteen on the Grange Hall's low-rise stage. They ran through that evening's playlist, rehearsed a few numbers they had not recently performed, and spent the rest of the afternoon wandering around the small town.

There wasn't much to see. Railroad tracks paralleled the state highway that bisected Quarryville. On the highway side were the town's main street, a small business district anchored by Quarryville Bank & Trust, and, once one moved away from the business district, the homes of the town's businessmen. On the far side of the railroad tracks were small, single-family homes constructed for quarry employees, and Quarry Road led past the workers' neighborhood out to the quarry. Before long, the musicians all returned to the hall and, at six o'clock, ladies from the Grange brought potluck dinner for everyone.

A few minutes before eight, having changed into their performance attire, the musicians settled into place behind their music stands and warmed up. At straight-up eight o'clock, Sonny took the stage, introduced himself, and welcomed the audience. As he turned to the band and counted off the beginning of the first number, a three-year-old Model B Ford Pickup rolled up to the Grange Hall's rear door with Elmer behind the wheel.

* * * *

Stan didn't tickle the keys so much as abuse them, but their audience that night either didn't notice or didn't care that the band's regular piano player never stepped foot on the stage. They danced to popular swing tunes, applauded appreciatively after every number, and the men in the audience seemed particularly enamored of Wanda each time she took the stage in her tight-fitting black dress.

At quarter past nine, a South Pacific freight train barreled through town, the rumble shaking even the Grange Hall three blocks from the track, and the sound of the train temporarily drowned out the band. Not knowing how long the train would interfere with their performance, the band continued, and they were halfway through the next number before the sound of the train faded into memory.

Just after nine-thirty, Wanda returned to the stage, leaned against Sonny, and whispered in his ear. "Carter's been shot."

Then she smiled at the audience and took her place behind the microphone. Without missing a beat, Sonny counted down the next tune, and Wanda mesmerized the audience once again.

When they finished the number, Sonny announced a short break, took Wanda's elbow, and escorted her off stage. The rest of the band had not been expecting a break until after the following number and murmured among themselves.

As Sonny and Wanda stepped backstage, Sonny asked, "Where is he?"

"In the bus."

"What happened?"

"They were caught," Wanda told him. They pushed through the stage door and climbed into the bus.

Carter lay on the rear seat, towels pressed against his abdomen, a grimace distorting his face and Bernie trying to comfort him.

"The train," Carter said. "You didn't tell us about the train. We might have gotten away, but—" Carter began coughing, a fine spray of blood misting the air above him.

Bernie took over the telling. "We were chased as we drove away from the payroll office. We might have made it, but the train cut us off. There was nowhere to go. We—Carter and me—we were in the back of the truck. The guy chasing us had us dead in his sights when Elmer came out shooting. Killed him, but not before he shot Carter."

"Elmer shot a cop?"

"Company man. A guard."

"Where'd Elmer get a gun?"

"Shotgun. From the truck he boosted."

"Where's Elmer now?"

"Dropped us here and took off. Said he'd get as far as he could before dumping the truck."

"And the money?"

Bernie used the tip of his shoe to nudge a canvas bag on the floor. "It's all here."

"What do we do now?" Wanda asked.

Sonny took a deep breath. "We finish the show as if nothing happened. You two take care of Carter."

He turned and headed out of the bus, and the rest of the band didn't question Sonny when he called them back to the stage for their last set, but they knew something had gone wrong because he slow counted the first number and rearranged the order of the remaining numbers so that Wanda did not return to the stage for her signature closing.

After the last note faded from the air, he encouraged the band to break down and pack the bus without hesitation. Then he hurried out the back and onto the bus to find that Carter had joined the celestial choir. Bernie lay on the floor beside him, a single shot through his forehead. Wanda, her suitcase, and the canvas bag containing the quarry's payroll were nowhere to be seen, and someone had rifled through Sonny's suitcase, taking the cash remaining from the band's previous crimes.

Sonny swore and slammed his hand against the back of one of the seats just as Heck Johnson, first trumpet, entered the bus carrying his music stand. Heck stopped when he saw the bodies in the back of the bus, and he turned to Sonny.

"Everything's gone south on us," Sonny said. "Let's just get everybody on board and get out of town."

He returned to the hall, collected the band's pay for the evening, and had everybody on the bus before word of a murder made its way across the tracks and long before anyone realized the quarry had been robbed.

Sonny drove, pushing the bus as fast as road conditions and his own inexperience behind the wheel allowed, and they were nearly an hour west of Quarryville when he had to stop because a Model B Ford Pickup blocked half the road, Elmer dead behind the wheel. Littering the ground around the truck were dozens of empty pay envelopes.

The musicians pushed the Ford out of the way, put Bernie's and Carter's bodies in the bed, and used gas siphoned from the truck's tank to douse the entire thing. Then they lit the truck on fire and drove away.

Sonny checked General Delivery in the next town on their route, discovered there was no mail awaiting him, and continued on to El Paso, where he expected to meet the advance man. He had enough money from the Quarryville gig to rent cheap rooms for the night, and after the musicians unloaded their belongings, Sonny cleaned the bus. He found, wedged behind the driver's seat, an envelope addressed to Wanda McDonald in care of General Delivery, Chicken Junction, Texas. The postmark on it matched the postmark on the package he'd picked up when the band overnighted there, and though no return address appeared on the envelope, the handwriting matched that of the band's advance man. Sonny folded the envelope in half and stuffed it into his shirt pocket.

That evening he took the band to dinner at a Mexican restaurant, told them he thought Andy and Wanda had taken off with their money, and divided the remaining cash from their final gig.

Some of the musicians had saved enough money to purchase bus tickets home, a few walked across the border into Ciudad Juarez hoping to pick up work performing in the gambling dens and whorehouses, and a few hocked their instruments rather than go too many days without eating. Two stuck up a grocery store and lit out of town in a stolen Chevrolet Sedan. Sonny sold the bus and bought a train ticket to Los Angeles.

* * * *

Having left four dead bodies behind in Texas, Sonny thought it wise to change his name when he reached California, and he stepped off the train as Steven Gable. He found work as a bandleader in a run-down nightclub, and he tried to parlay his fading good looks into a movie career by spending his days making the rounds of the movie studios looking for work.

That's where he saw Wanda six years after the Quarryville payroll job. She was exiting the RKO Studios lot, and he had just finished auditioning for a three-line role in a crime picture. Her red hair had been bleached blond and cut short, and she wore a form-fitting white dress that would make an A-lister jealous, but there was no mistaking who she was. He caught her elbow. "Wanda?"

She turned and gave him a quick once-over. He wore a battered fedora and a trench coat over a cheap suit, having dressed as best he could to look like the alcoholic detective role for which he had auditioned. "I'm sorry," she said, "but you must have mistaken me for someone else."

The look in her eyes told him otherwise, and he said, "How about if we go for a drink? I know a quiet place a couple of blocks from here."

Wanda's eyes widened when she recognized his voice. She lowered her voice to a near whisper. "Get away from me, Sonny, or I'll scream."

He squeezed her elbow and saw her wince. "Do you really want to draw that much attention? Do you want to explain that mess back in Texas to some studio rent-a-cop who might be money hungry enough to turn you in for the reward?"

"I—" she started. "There's a reward?"

Sonny nodded.

"How do I know you won't turn me in?"

"I don't have any reason to," he said. "Not yet, anyhow."

She didn't resist when he gave her arm a tug, and they walked two blocks to a bar frequented by B-listers and wannabes. Sonny directed his band's former singer to a darkened booth in the back, where they sat opposite each other and ordered gin straight up from an aging actress whose squeaky voice kept her from making the transition from silent films to talkies.

After they had their drinks and Sonny was certain they would not be interrupted, he told her about finding the envelope addressed to her in their advance man's handwriting and asked, "Why did you shoot Bernie?"

"I didn't. Andy did."

"So where's Andy now?"

She smiled. "He disappeared."

"And the money?"

"Gone," she said. "A girl has expenses."

"The clothes? The hair?"

"Yes," she said. "All of that. And more. It didn't last a year, but it lasted six months longer than Andy."

"So why did you do it? Why did you stab us all in the back like that?"

"The Quarryville payroll job was the biggest haul the band ever raked in, and Andy knew it would be when he set it up," Wanda explained. "There was enough money to last the two of us a good while but split twenty-one ways it wouldn't have lasted at all. You know how long Andy waited for a score like that?"

"Just as long as the rest of us," Sonny said. "So how'd he do it?"

"No one's ever seen Andy but me and you, so he was waiting behind the Grange Hall to rob the musicians when they rolled in. He didn't anticipate the guard and the train. That was just a mess. Elmer dumped Carter and Bernie and the money and took off before Andy could do anything, and he was watching when I went into the hall to get you. After you went back in, I tore through your suitcase looking for the other money I knew you had. Andy joined us on the bus, saw that Carter had bought the farm by then, and shot Bernie. No witnesses. That's what Andy said."

"And Elmer?"

"Found him on the side of the road. That truck he heisted had blown a tire—or maybe that guard shot it, I don't know—but I made Andy stop. Elmer must have figured out what was going on. He pointed a shotgun at Andy, so Andy shot him—shot him and left him."

"But you took the time to empty the pay envelopes?"

She nodded. "Andy said we should leave behind everything but the money, so that's what we did."

"The band broke up after that," Sonny told her. "We could have continued without you, but we didn't have the money to continue, and we didn't have an advance man to book our gigs."

"I'm sorry about that," Wanda said, her demeanor having changed while she was talking through the events of that night in Quarryville, "but those are the breaks. If they're really looking for me, they're looking for a red-headed singer, but they won't find me. I'm not a redhead anymore, and I don't sing."

"That's too bad," Sonny told her.

"That it?" she asked. "You want to put your hand up my skirt for old-time's sake, or can I go?"

Wanda didn't wait for an answer and slid out of the booth. Sonny tried to follow her, but the waitress stopped him with a hand to his chest.

"Cop or no cop," she squeaked. "You ain't paid for the drinks."

By the time Sonny sorted out the tab and reached the sidewalk, Wanda was gone.

* * * *

He caught the streetcar and returned to his one-bedroom apartment, where he thumbed through the telephone directory looking for Wanda Mc-Donald or W. McDonald until he realized she had likely changed her name as well as her look. Then he paced the living room until it was time to prepare for his show at Café Monroe.

The musicians were a motley crew of has-beens and never-wases who could carry a tune when they weren't drunk or jacked up on junk, and Sonny—as Steven Gable—did his best to keep the audience entertained through the evening even though few couples ever graced the dance floor.

After the show, while the musicians were packing away their instruments, he sat on the edge of the stage nursing three fingers of gin and talking with Jerzy Kerkowski, the band's pug-faced drummer.

"How do I find a woman?"

"You got enough scratch, at least three of the cigarette girls will go home with you."

"I'm not looking for that."

"What are you looking for?"

"Revenge."

Jerzy looked at him. "What'd she do, steal your heart?"

"Worse." Sonny finished his gin, stood, and walked into the night.

* * * *

"This woman you're looking for, she an actress?" Hiram Goldman asked.

Sonny shrugged. "I saw her coming out of the RKO lot."

Hiram was an assistant in the casting department, and he had been the one to tip Sonny off about the alcoholic detective role. He dropped a thick pile of 8"x10" glossy photographs on the desk between them. "Blondes with a bob," he said. "These are all I have."

Sonny carefully examined each photograph and shook his head each time he flipped one over. When he finished without finding Wanda, he asked, "Could she be an employee?"

"You'd have to talk to personnel about that."

Personnel turned out to be a bust, and so did conversations with some of the musicians who performed for movie club scenes. Talking to the guards paid off.

Sonny was hired for the role of the alcoholic detective, spent one day on set reciting his three lines and was stopped by one of the studio guards as he left the lot that afternoon.

"That blonde you're looking for," the guard said. "I think I saw her the other day in the back seat of a limo."

"You get the license number?"

"I did one better," the guard said. "I had a friend at the DMV run it for me."

He held out a slip of paper and Sonny took it from him. The name written on it—Dimitri Soros—meant nothing, but under it was an address. Sonny handed the guard a crumpled five dollar bill.

That night he bought a map of Los Angeles, and the next morning he stuck the map in one pocket of his jacket and his .38 in the other. He rode the trolley as far as he could and walked the last mile to the address on the paper.

He found himself on the porch of a two-story Georgian mansion fronted by an expanse of lawn large enough to graze several head of cattle. He rang the bell and waited patiently until Wanda opened the door. She wore a silk robe, cinched tight at the waist, that emphasized a figure that was still buxom and wide-hipped.

She grabbed his arm and pulled him inside. "I saw you from the bedroom window, Sonny. What the hell are you doing here?"

"I didn't believe that sob story you fed me the other day. You said the money's gone, but one look at this place tells me it ain't."

"None of this is mine," she insisted.

"Then whose is it?"

Andy Stewart joined them from the den. He wore a smoking jacket and a wry smile. "Wanda said she ran into you."

Sonny stared at Wanda. "You said the money lasted six months longer than Andy."

Andy held out his hand, "Dimitri Soros, producer."

Sonny didn't take it.

"This is the land of make-believe," Andy said as he lowered his hand and slipped it into the pocket of his smoking jacket. "Out here you can be anybody you want to be, but you, you're just a two-bit band leader for a rundown nightclub chasing bit parts at minor studios."

Sonny pulled the .38 from his waistband and pointed it at Wanda. "I want what's mine. I want what you took from me."

"Oh, Sonny," Wanda said. "We didn't take anything that belonged to you."

He swung the gun toward Andy. "You took everything from me. Both of you did. Now it's time to give it back."

"You think your life deserves an encore, Sonny?" Andy asked. "Another shot at the big time? You were already on your way down by the time you reached Quarryville. You were lucky I could get gigs for you and your band of losers."

"With that money we could have—"

"We made something of ourselves, Sonny," Wanda said as Sonny turned the revolver on her again. "You never would have."

"You killed four people to do it."

"Two," Andy corrected. "The other two—"

Sonny turned the .38 on Andy again. "So, what's two more?"

"You shoot us, then what'll you have?" Andy asked. "You certainly won't have the money, and you won't ever have anything like this." He swept his hand in a circle to indicate the Georgian mansion he shared with Wanda.

"I'll go to the cops, tell them what you did in Texas."

"And you'll go down with us," Andy said. "You were the mastermind behind everything."

"Let's face it," Wanda said, "if one of us rats out the others, we all go down for the killings, and ain't none of us ready for the hot seat."

Andy lit a cigarette and thought for a moment. "There's another way."

"Which is?"

"I was your advance man, finding you gigs all across the southwest. How about I do the same for you here?"

"You want to be my agent?"

"Not exactly. I'm backing a picture at Monogram that needs a band leader. Two nightclub numbers, a dozen lines. I can put in a good word with the casting director."

Sonny lowered the .38 and slipped it into his jacket pocket. "You can get me that?"

"I can get you in the door, but you have to deliver the goods."

"Let me pour some drinks," Wanda said, "so we can toast your good fortune. I have something here that'll make you forget that cheap gin you favor."

She poured three fingers of scotch for each of them, Andy made a toast, and then he left Sonny with Wanda while he went into the den to make a phone call. Wanda settled on the couch, and when her robe parted to reveal a long length of well-tanned leg, she was slow to cover it.

"You two on the up-and-up now?" Sonny asked.

"Straight arrows," she said. "And Andy—you'd better get used to calling him Dimitri or Mr. Soros—has the juice to make things happen."

As if on cue, Andy returned from the den and handed Sonny his business card with a note handwritten on the back. "It's all set. Your audition is set for eleven a.m. tomorrow. Go to the Monogram lot, ask the guard to direct you to the casting director for *Downbeat Deadbeat,* and show him this."

Sonny finished his drink, returned to town, and used the last of his cash to buy a new tuxedo. He wore it to the club that evening, and Jerzy Kerkowski stopped him when he walked in through the back door of Café Monroe. "Why the new duds?"

"I found her," Sonny said.

"You get your revenge?"

"Better," Sonny said. "I got my encore."

Michael Bracken is the author of several books, including the private eye novel *All White Girls*, and more than 1,300 short stories in several genres. His short crime fiction has appeared in *Alfred Hitchcock's Mystery Magazine, Ellery Queen's Mystery Magazine, The Best American Mystery Stories,* and in many other anthologies and periodicals. Additionally, Bracken has edited several anthologies, including the Anthony Award-nominated *The Eyes of Texas,* the three-volume *Fedora* series, and the *Mickey Finn* series. He and his wife, Temple, reside in Central Texas.

SWITCH AND BAIT

CYNTHIA WARD

PENOBSCOT BAY, MAINE, MARCH 13, 1978, 9:31 P.M.

"Ain't we lucky that miserable bastid's got a private dock we can pull right up to," Chase Hayes remarked to his wife and sternman.

He killed the diesel engine of the *Stormy Sally* (his dad's old wooden boat, named after Chase's mother), and they got busy tying up the lobster smack.

"Whole property's dark," Bethany observed. "Guess Billy Bolduc and his old lady *did* take their kids to the John Denver concert, down to Portland. God knows how they got tickets. I heerd them concerts sold out in an hour even when they booked a second show."

"God knows how they *afforded* them tickets, when they got so many kids," Chase said. "Billy's wife ain't even Catholic, but she pumps one out every year."

"What do you expect, when she married a Frenchman?" Bethany said. "Anyways, that frog'll come home to a lesson he won't soon forget."

"Billy ain't showed any signs of a memory so far," Chase said. "We've knotted his trap lines, we've cut 'em, and he's still droppin his lobster pots in our territory and everyone else's."

In the starlight, Chase and Bethany picked up their baseball bats and walked up the dock, avoiding patches of ice. The weathered wood took them over restless waves that broke on a rocky beach. The granite was shaggy with bladderwrack and looked like a jumble of decapitated hippie heads.

Several yards beyond the beach, an old two-story house stood in front of a low ridge that was covered with white pines. Last winter, the Bolducs had inherited the house, along with a hundred acres of shore-front property and a lobster smack, from Billy's father-in-law.

The chilly night air held a suggestion of pine resin as Chase and Bethany cautiously made their way around the shadowed house and windowless outbuilding. The shed was covered with bare shingles, gray from years of exposure, and the lobster buoy on one wall had rough areas, like clumps of barnacles, where the paint had been gouged. The white paint on the house was cracked, and mold streaked the cupped clapboards.

The buildings were dark, but the couple peeked through every window on the first floor of the house.

Then they started up the ridge. Avoiding patches of snow, they kept to the crumbling edge of the hot-top driveway that proceeded gradually up the slope. Eventually the ground leveled and the trees ended at a two-lane highway. The moon was a fingernail clipping above the blueberry barrens that rose to the west. There wasn't a building in sight, and the road was pale and empty in the starlight.

"Ain't nobody on the whole damn property," Chase concluded.

"Ayuh," Bethany said. "Billy's pickup and his wife's Dodge are both gone."

Chase hefted his baseball bat. "Lesson time."

They retraced their steps. As they neared the base of the slope, the house appeared among the pines.

"I'll take care of this side of the house," Chase murmured, "if you'll go round to the ocean side and do your part."

Bethany went around the corner and Chase shattered the nearest bedroom window with his baseball bat.

It was quite a surprise to Chase when a bright light flashed in the room and something grazed his left shoulder like the edge of a top maul, accompanied by the crack of a rifle.

Chase hadn't finished ducking before Billy Bolduc was leaning through the broken window. A stray beam of starlight gleamed on his grin and the barrel of his Remington .30-06.

"Figured you'd come sneakin around here tonight, you son of a whore," he said to Chase. "Well, I didn't go with my fambly to Portland, and I hid my Ford in the spruce up the highway. And since you're tresspassin, I'm within my rights"—Billy aimed his rifle at Chase's right eye—"to kill you."

Bethany came around the corner, rubber boots silent on the fallen pine needles, and her baseball bat connected as solidly with Billy's skull as a Yaz swing meeting a pitch.

After a few moments of watching the man lie as limply over the windowsill as a drape, Chase muttered, "Billy ain't movin."

"He landed on broken glass stickin up like knives, but he ain't bled a drop, neither," Bethany observed.

They checked Billy for a breath or heartbeat.

Finally, Bethany said, "Numbnut went and got himself killed."

"Well," Chase said, "we'd better come up with an alibi, or it won't matter that he started it. We'll be doin life at Thomaston."

"Oh, the bay's choppy, and you know how fussy that ol' engine can be," Bethany said. "We got delayed comin back from emptyin our pots. Happens all the time."

"Well," Chase said, "that won't necessarily be enough, if nobody else whose territory he's been poachin on was out at this time a night."

Bethany grinned. "Who says we're leavin that worthless bastid's body here for his fambly to find? Grab the other end and we'll get him on the *Stormy Sally*. We'll sink him where nobody'd ever think to look."

"And check back from time to time," Chase said.

"Ayuh," Bethany said. "Billy'll finally serve a useful purpose."

"As lobster bait."

AUTHOR'S NOTE

Special thanks to Kevin Hamor for information on lobster fishing.

Cynthia Ward has published stories in *Analog*, *Asimov's*, *Nightmare*, *Weird Tales*, and other magazines and anthologies. She edited *Lost Trails: Forgotten Tales of the Weird West* Volumes One and Two. With Nisi Shawl, Cynthia co-created the ground-breaking Writing the Other writers' workshop and coauthored the diversity fiction-writing handbook, *Writing the Other: A Practical Approach*, which were honored with the 2020 Locus Special Award. Her latest short novel, *Golden Woman: Blood-Thirsty Agent Book 4*, will be released by Aqueduct Press in Fall 2021.

BECOMING ZERO

JAMES A. HEARN

Texas oil executive Roger Dubose was dead. The medical examiner had ruled his sudden demise as "natural," and to any outside observer, this was true.

But Professor Arnold Pugmire knew the truth: it had been murder. A perfect murder, with thousands of accessories who told no tales.

After the last guest departed Dubose's wake, Pugmire closed the front door to the Dubose mansion and giggled. What a magnificent day it had been! Feeling the press of Amanda Dubose's hand as they'd listened to her husband's eulogy. Seeing Dubose's coffin lowered into a dark grave. Listening to condolences during the wake.

Laughing again, Pugmire locked the front door and went looking for Amanda. He found the widow in her library, lounging on a divan by a gas fireplace. Pugmire stood in the room's threshold to admire the view. In the firelight, her hair was spun gold, the sinuous curves of her black dress shimmering like the carapace of an Egyptian scarab. She was thirty-three, attractive, and slim while he was balding, middle-aged, and plump...a man accustomed to indulging his appetites.

Except for one.

"I'm married, Arnie," she'd always said. "We can never be more than friends."

Friend was such a loathsome word to a man in love. How long should a widow grieve a husband? Even one as loathsome as Dubose? Surely not more than six months?

A floorboard creaked beneath his ponderous weight, causing Amanda to flinch.

"Arnie?"

Pugmire walked to the back of the divan, his hand inches from Amanda's left shoulder. He licked his lips at the gooseflesh prickling her flawless skin.

"Are you cold, my dear?" he asked.

"I just felt a chill. Is everyone gone?"

"We're alone." *Finally.*

"He didn't come," sighed Amanda, crestfallen.

Pugmire's eyelids fluttered. "Who didn't?"

"Craig Connors."

Despite his girth, Pugmire practically sprang to the other side of the divan. He sat down beside her. "The private detective? You no longer need Connors to prove Roger's infidelity, and the prenuptial agreement can't hurt you now. All of this is yours," said Pugmire. He made a sweeping gesture that seemed to encompass the whole of the world.

"Craig was doing much more than documenting Roger's trysts."

There was a smoldering glint in Amanda's blue eyes, and Pugmire's mouth twisted in distaste at the honeyed way she'd said "Craig." In the interview to hire Connors, Pugmire had seen the way Amanda's gaze lingered on the younger man. It was a look she'd never bestowed on him.

The detective wasn't a natural athlete like Roger Dubose, but the native Texan exuded confidence and strength. His keen brown eyes seemed to see everything, and the square of his jawline looked like it would break any fist that dared to strike it.

To top it off, Connors was ex-military and a decorated sniper. A killer! Where another man might hang a diploma in his office, the detective proudly displayed combat medals and certificates of service.

Pugmire had counseled Amanda to hire someone else—anyone else— but it was too late. Connors had his hooks in.

"Since when did you and *Craig* get on a first-name basis?" asked Pugmire.

Amanda's voice was flat. "He's just a friend."

Pugmire grimaced at the word. "A friend who can't be bothered with funerals."

"Craig has other clients, I'm sure."

Amanda's phone chimed. She glanced at it hopefully, sighed, and put it away.

"Connors?" asked Pugmire.

"Nobody important. Another text offering condolences."

Pugmire took her phone and set it on the coffee table. "Anyone who voluntarily joins the military is desperate or a fool. Why'd you hire him?"

"Because he's the best. Now be a pet and bring me a whiskey."

Like a Pavlovian dog, Pugmire rose to obey. Along the way to the wet bar, he nearly tripped on a Persian rug that cost more than his Volvo. He tsked to himself. The home of oil executive Roger Dubose was a study in American corporate greed run amok. Why did executives live like kings when their intellectual superiors in academia, the keepers of the flame of knowledge, got by on scraps?

In life, Dubose had the best of everything. The swimming pool behind his Hill Country mansion was bigger than Pugmire's townhouse, with an infinity edge overlooking the winding Colorado River and Austin skyline.

But the greatest prize Dubose had ever acquired was Amanda Michelle

O'Brien. Somehow, the greedy bastard had landed a trophy wife *before* making his millions.

Pugmire handed Amanda a whiskey and sat back down beside her.

She fixed her red-rimmed blue eyes on him and said, "I introduced you to Roger in this room. Remember the faculty Christmas party?"

Pugmire remembered every encounter he'd ever had with Amanda. He lived for the cordial hugs that seemed to linger beyond politeness, the admiring glances she gave him when he talked politics. "You were relating how you'd met Roger."

"The UCLA freshman mixer."

To hear Amanda tell it, they'd stood next to each other for ten minutes before Dubose, his voice quavering, broke the ice. Without preamble, he talked about the Environment, with a capital E, and how he hoped to work for the Sierra Club. The two shy freshmen had left together, talking into the wee hours of the morning.

"Roger swept me off my feet," said Amanda wistfully. "He was a competitive swimmer, long and lean. Ambitious, but poor. Daddy didn't approve, of course. He forbade our marriage and threatened to cut me off. Roger stood up to him, offering to sign a prenuptial agreement if it would secure my inheritance. Daddy agreed."

Pugmire felt bile stinging his throat. Was she forgetting her loveless marriage? How she'd cried on Pugmire's shoulder whenever Dubose went on a "business trip" with his bimbo secretary?

Amanda patted Pugmire's arm. "Roger was an environmentalist back then. Not the gun-loving neo-con you knew." She polished off her drink. "I suppose it was partially my fault we drifted apart. Roger gave up his job at the Sierra Club when I was accepted to graduate school at UT. He didn't even know I'd applied."

Pugmire had heard this story as well. When she'd announced the exciting opportunity to study poetry in Austin, Dubose had flown into a rage. Did she expect him to leave his dream job, not to mention his ailing parents, for dead poets?

Apparently she did.

Dubose had relented. After all, was his run-of-the-mill job—as Amanda had put it to him—worth stifling her creativity? And as for his aging parents, rest homes made better caregivers than children.

"I loved Austin's progressive culture, carefree spirit, and live music festivals. But the Hill Country was a punishment for Roger." Amanda seemed to be talking to herself as much as to Pugmire. "He loved the trees and the outdoors, but suffered terribly from seasonal allergies, especially cedar. He spent a fortune on pills and neti pots. He looked so funny, bending over the sink and—"

"Coming to Austin was the right decision," interjected Pugmire. "I'd never have met you. And the world would've been deprived of your poetry."

"So true."

Pugmire, a microbiologist, couldn't tell a simile from a metaphor. Amanda's poetry didn't even rhyme, but he supposed that had something to do with elevating substance over style.

"You always know how to cheer me up, Arnie. Fetch me another drink?"

Pugmire returned to the wet bar and made two drinks. "Roger was a hypocrite. How could an 'environmentalist' ever take a job at an oil company?"

"He did that to spite me for dragging him away from his dying parents."

"As if marriage made them your burdens."

Pugmire sat back down, and Amanda placed a hand on his knee. "Did I cry like a baby when they found Daddy floating in his swimming pool after his company went bankrupt? No. I sucked it up, even though the financial security blanket I'd had all my life was gone. And as my husband rose to CFO at Paramount Oil, the prenuptial agreement designed to protect me could now leave me penniless."

"You're safe." Pugmire clumsily slipped his arm behind Amanda's shoulders, his sausage-thick fingers brushing her skin.

She got up and stood before the fireplace. Gas flames crackled against ceramic logs in a blaze that never consumed. Though an atheist, Pugmire found himself thinking of devils roasting sinners in eternal hellfire.

"Do you think Roger suffered overmuch?" she asked.

Pugmire nearly crushed the glass in his hand. How many times had she wished her husband dead while he wiped her tears? He gathered himself. "I don't think so."

It was a lie. Primary amebic meningoencephalitis, an extremely rare brain infection brought on by *Naegleria fowleri*, was no doubt extremely painful. The amoebas that caused PAM, found in bodies of fresh water in warm climates, migrated from the sinuses into the frontal lobes of the brain, where they fed.

What had it been like for Dubose, Pugmire wondered, who'd gone to bed thinking he'd a mild case of flu? The frontal lobes were involved in motor function, problem solving, memory, and language. As the hungry amoebas divided and conquered, did they literally eat Dubose's memories? As his brain swelled and hemorrhaged, did he lose himself, one synapse at a time, before lapsing into a fatal coma?

Pugmire would've given anything to see the blood oozing from Dubose's liquefied brain via the ears, nose, and mouth. Then a ghastly thought occurred to Pugmire. Did the amoebas feed even now, pseudopods engulfing prey inside a dead host?

"Where did he get those," began Amanda, "what did the doctors call them?"

Pugmire scowled. What was the point of rehashing the subject? "*Naegleria fowleri*. He must've contracted PAM at the lake house." The lake house was Dubose's escape from the cares of life, including his wife. He'd been known to kayak in all weather, despite his allergies. "Roger probably slipped off the kayak and water got in his nose."

Amanda nodded thoughtfully. "Roger woke up with a headache the Thursday after his trip." She was speaking in the clear voice she used when reciting her poems, Pugmire noted. "He was running a fever, with nausea and muscular aches. I told him to go to the doctor, but he just laughed and said he'd shake it off. I even offered to skip my conference in Chicago." She paused, as if for effect. "When I came back home Monday, he was sprawled in bed, the sheets twisted and bloody. It was the shock of my life."

Pugmire gaped at the regret in her voice. Had he misinterpreted Amanda's half-promises of love, her lingering touches? Hadn't her every action, ever since they'd met, led to his *grand gesture*?

That's how he thought of Dubose's death. Not murder. Murder was an act of violence. Killing Dubose was an act of love...love he was now free to declare. Who cared what the world might think? Convention and so-called morality were for the weak-minded.

Pugmire cleared his throat, but Amanda's buzzing cell phone interrupted him.

"It's a text from Craig!" she said in delight.

Quick as a snake, Pugmire rose and snatched the phone from her grasp.

"Arnie! Give that back." There was a note of panic in her voice.

Pugmire read the message: *Get rid of him. I need to talk to you about Roger's death. I'll be there in ten minutes.*

How'd Connors know he was here? Pugmire glanced furtively at the security camera above the fireplace.

Are you watching us, Connors?

Amanda was reaching for her phone, but Pugmire kept her at bay. He suddenly remembered the supposed condolences from "nobody important" earlier in the evening, and scrolled through her texts to this message: *Authorized user Craig Connors has accessed your home surveillance network.*

"Give me my phone!"

"Call him," said Pugmire. "Tell him to stay away."

Amanda crossed her arms. "You need to leave, Arnold."

"Why? So you can be with him?"

Pugmire's ears rang from her resounding slap. He held a hand to his cheek, surprised to find it wet with tears.

"Arnie, forgive me," said Amanda as she took his other hand.

Pugmire's heart skipped a beat. It was worth the slap to feel the touch of those fingers. "My love, this is your last chance. It's either him or me."

She let go of his hand. "You don't decide who my other friends are."

Pugmire grabbed her wrist and pulled her close. "Friends? Is that all I am to you? Would a friend have done—" He stopped abruptly, remembering the security camera.

"Would a friend have done what?"

Pugmire's eyes narrowed. *She knows! And she wants me to confess it on camera…for Connors to hear.* "Amanda, how could you throw away all we have?"

Amanda wrenched her wrist from his grip. "There is no 'we' and never will be. Get out."

Get out get out get out…

The echoing words swelled to bursting in Pugmire's brain. Shapes swam in his vision, like tiny amoebas crisscrossing his optic nerves. His beautiful dream was slipping away, all because of Connors! He took a deep, steadying breath.

"Kiss me before I go," said Pugmire.

"Arnie…"

"Just once. A lover's kiss, from your soul to mine."

"One kiss?"

"And you'll never see me again."

Amanda's lips curved in a wry smile. She stepped forward, her face inches from his. Pugmire took her in his arms.

At first, her mouth was closed, her body unresponsive. Wooden. But then her lips opened, and he kissed her deeply. To his shock, she kissed him back. It was the most glorious moment of his life.

But she'd chosen Connors! This was a kiss goodbye, not one of new beginnings. Whatever humanity was left in Dr. Arnold Pugmire contracted, shrinking down to microscopic size. His arms were not arms, but amorphous extensions of a mindless body.

His mouth sucked down her very breath as he squeezed, as if engulfing her very soul. Amanda Dubose wriggled uselessly in his grasp, and he heard her ribs crack.

* * * *

Craig Connors sat in his office, a drink in his hands, and studied the coroner's report on Roger Dubose's death. He'd gotten a copy from a friend at the medical examiner's office. Something didn't add up, but he wasn't sure what.

It came back to his client Amanda Dubose, the sultry college professor who'd hired him to document her husband's trysts. Connors hadn't talked to her since the night they'd made love, nor had he gone to her husband's funeral.

If Connors had learned one thing from all the cheap dime-store detective novels he'd read as a kid, it was this: never become personally involved with a client. It clouded the judgment when a man might need his wits to stay alive.

Those crime writers had never met Amanda Dubose.

The woman had gotten under Connors's skin. She reminded him of the ubiquitous sand of Afghanistan's Registan Desert, how it found its way into every crevice of the body, chafing the skin raw no matter what gear you wore or how often you washed. In the desert, you surrendered to the sand or you went crazy.

It'd started the moment she walked into his office, Arnold Pugmire in tow. Connors knew better than to call it love at first sight. But it was damn close.

"I think my husband's going to divorce me," Amanda had told Connors.

She'd looked like the best kind of client: rich. The Mercedes she'd driven that day was easily a hundred grand, and the South Sea pearls at her throat looked just as expensive.

"What makes you think so?"

"Roger's moving around his money and won't tell me why. My checking account is drying up."

"What's he do for a living?" asked Connors.

"He's the CFO of Paramount Oil and rich as Croesus."

Connors whistled. He had sudden visions of cracking open a beer on a fully paid-off bass boat.

"Croesus," began Pugmire in a lecturing tone, "was the king of—"

"I know who Croesus was," said Connors. "What do you do, Mrs. Dubose?"

"I'm an English professor and a poet."

"Surely you've heard of her?" asked Pugmire.

Connors ignored the question. "Mrs. Dubose, is your husband faithful?"

"No."

Connors nodded to himself. "You've got the upper hand. Assuming you aren't, ahem." He cleared his throat and glanced at Pugmire.

Amanda giggled at the implication. "Arnie's a friend from work. A professor of microbiology."

Beside her, Pugmire flinched.

Connors tried not to smile at the man's discomfiture. There was something between these two professors, something twisted and unbalanced. "The best strategy is to file first. Get the high ground. I know some great divorce attorneys."

Amanda shook her head. She went on to explain that a divorce would be ruinous given her prenuptial agreement, signed at a time when Amanda had been a would-be heiress and Dubose didn't have two dimes to rub together. Then Amanda's family fortune dried up, while Dubose rose to power at Paramount Oil. Amanda finished this tale of woe by telling the detective she was convinced her husband was up to something illegal, with his secret business meetings and unexplained money transfers.

Connors steepled his fingers. "Better and better. With Roger in prison, you could gain control over his assets, then divorce him at your leisure."

"Will you help me, Craig?"

He'd almost said no, for reasons he couldn't explain. It was the same feeling he'd get back in the desert, when the way forward seemed perfectly clear. That's when a roadside bomb would shatter the quiet in a rain of blood and bone.

When she'd removed her strand of pearls and set them on the desk, Connors agreed to take the case.

The money was good, the job seemingly routine: document Dubose's infidelity and uncover the hidden assets or illegal activity.

Connors set to work, installing GPS trackers on Dubose's vehicles and cracking the passwords for his voicemail, email, and online accounts. Amanda had even given him remote access to the security cameras in their palatial mansion and their lake house.

For the next six weeks, Dubose was always at the tips of Connors's fingers. Like a cadaver beneath a dissecting scalpel, Dubose's life was flayed open, layer by layer.

At first, Connors thought of his mark as a fool. What man would run around on a woman like Amanda? She was sexy, smart, and funny. A little pretentious, but what professor wasn't?

But the more Connors followed Dubose, the more he felt sorry for the man. He suffered silently through whatever indignities Amanda heaped on him, never raising his voice. He asked about her poetry and her classes. He even enquired after his mother-in-law, suffering with terminal Alzheimer's back in California.

Dubose's "hidden asset"—the supposed illegal activity Amanda had hoped to uncover—turned out to be a private charity dedicated to alternative energy, a secret from his oil company.

Except for his infidelity, Dubose was a veritable saint. The other woman in his life wasn't some pretty young underling, as it was with so many cheating executives. Alice Gibbons was a fifty-year-old widower who liked Willie Nelson, smoked Camels, and had an infectious laugh. More than once, Connors had caught himself laughing out loud at one of Alice's ribald jokes.

As the case progressed, Connors found himself neglecting Dubose's pedestrian comings and goings. He was either at work or at his lake house with Alice. Even his sneezes and nasal sprays seemed as predictable as clockwork.

It was more interesting to check on Amanda in the Dubose mansion, via their security system. At first it was little things, like watching her make a smoothie. Was that kale she was adding, or spinach?

Pugmire would show up occasionally to have dinner or listen to poetry. It was clear the guy worshipped her, and it was equally clear that it would never, ever come to anything. Connors would've felt sorry for him if he weren't such an ass.

Three weeks into the case, things took an unexpected turn. Connors was in the office working on a missing person case, when he'd looked up to find Amanda sunbathing by her pool. She'd positioned her lounge chair in full view of a security camera.

Connors was about to phone another client, but when she took off her top and began applying suntan lotion, Connors hung up the phone and just watched.

From that day, the high-definition cameras followed her every move-ment, from her exercise room where she did Pilates, to the pool where she sunbathed, to the bedroom where she undressed. Sometimes, Connors swore Amanda was staring straight through the cameras, *looking at him* looking at her.

It had gotten so bad Connors would leave his laptop at the office, just so he wouldn't be tempted to spy on her after hours.

When the evidence against Dubose had been gathered—photographs, recordings, financial statements—and presented to Amanda at her mansion, her face drained of color.

Connors could still recall her trembling voice.

"Alice Gibbons," she'd said in cold fury. "He's been cheating on me with her? She's ancient!"

Connors said nothing.

"What's he see in her?"

Plenty, Connors thought. A woman who made you laugh was worth her weight in gold. Plus, Alice was a curvaceous woman with an appetite for bar-becue from joints that had never been featured on Food Network…a woman after his own heart.

"He can't possibly be in love with her."

"Certainly not," Connors lied. He went on to tell her that Dubose's hid-den asset was a renewable energy charity, not some nefarious scheme. So much for sending him to prison.

"Craig, there must be something you've overlooked."

"Your husband isn't a bad guy. Believe me, I've tracked plenty who were worse. Maybe with some professional help, you could patch things up."

Connors couldn't believe he was telling her this. Not for the first time, he imagined a future where Amanda divorced Dubose. Was it so farfetched to believe a professor would fall for an average Joe like him?

"Patch things up? He's a gun-loving, greedy bastard and a cheater! His company's killing the planet!"

Connors was about to reply that her boat-like Mercedes had one hell of a carbon footprint, but he kept his mouth shut.

"If you want the rest of your exorbitant fee, Craig Connors, you'll find something I can use as leverage!"

In a few moments, Amanda had gone from worldly college professor, cool and collected, to the aging starlet from *Sunset Boulevard*.

Connors shuddered when, "As you wish," slipped out of his mouth. Had she turned him into a man who'd do anything she asked?

At the mansion's doorway, just as Connors was thinking he'd escaped with his personal and professional honor intact, Amanda had flung herself on him with wild abandon. Later that night, as he lay in Amanda's bed with her head on his shoulder, she'd talked about killing.

As Connors sat at his desk looking over the coroner's report on Roger Dubose, he went over the conversation in his mind, point by point.

"You're not like other men I've been with, Craig."

In the darkness, Connors's eyes snapped open. Her voice had a drugged, dream-like quality.

"Oh?"

"You've killed people."

"I was a sniper. It's in the job description."

"I'm serious. Most men I know are academics. They're not men of action. I doubt any of them have held a gun."

There was something about the way she said "gun" that was dirty. Pornographic.

"Men like Pugmire? You know he's hopelessly in love with you?"

"Of course. But Arnie's not like you." Amanda twirled a finger lazily through his chest hair, and Connors felt himself stir. "What's it like to kill a man?"

Connors pulled away, suddenly deflated and uncomfortable in the satin sheets of Roger Dubose's bed. Amanda reached out with a claw-like hand and restrained his arm.

"Tell me."

His reasons for answering were dark, obscured from his mind. "It's the zero."

"Go on."

Connors sank back into the bed. "There's a barrier between life and death, thin and fragile as a soap bubble. The merest pinprick, and the bubble bursts." He snapped his trigger finger against his thumb.

"What's the zero?"

"A proper kill is done mechanically, without emotion. Just as you've practiced on the range ten thousand times. You aren't on a rooftop in some foreign country, hungry and tired, feeling the sun bake your brain in your helmet. You aren't even a Marine charged with keeping your platoon safe as they complete their mission. You aren't you, and the man in the crosshairs isn't a man."

"He's a target," she supplied.

Connors nodded grimly. "You become a zero, and so does he. You squeeze the trigger, and the bullet pricks the bubble."

"Pop." She gripped his arm tighter. "But that's war. You're licensed to carry. Have you ever killed someone for…personal reasons?"

Connors didn't answer as he wrested his arm from her grasp. What was she asking? Did she want the dirt on her husband, or did she want him *under* the dirt?

The office line rang, bringing Connors back to the present. It was Dr. Ramsey Stewart from the Travis County Medical Examiner's Office, returning his call. The doctor's voice was animated, almost giddy, to discuss how freshwater amoebas had entered Roger Dubose's brain via the sinus cavity and turned his frontal lobes to jelly. When Connors asked about the speed of infection, the doctor replied that it had happened very quickly, within seven days.

Connors muttered a goodbye and hung up the phone.

Seven days? If Dr. Stewart was right, Dubose had been infected during his most recent kayaking trip. Connors had surveilled the excursion from his office, via his link to the lake house's security system.

Dubose had been with Alice. They'd stayed inside all weekend, binge-watching Netflix and making love, in between Dubose's bouts of sneezing and nasal sprays. If he never went kayaking, how'd he contract PAM?

Sweat popped out on Connors's brow. It wasn't a question of how. It was a question of who…and the answer was Dr. Arnold Pugmire, the microbiologist.

Pugmire could've cultivated amoebas. But how'd he administer them? In Dubose's nasal spray?

Connors flipped open his laptop. He connected remotely to the Dubose mansion's monitoring system and found himself looking at Amanda. She was sitting in her library, Pugmire lurking behind her.

Amanda turned toward the man. "He didn't come."

"Who didn't?" asked Pugmire.

"Craig Connors."

Connors kept listening as he raced to his pickup, laptop in hand.

* * * *

Arnold Pugmire sat by the pool and stared blankly at the skyscrapers of downtown Austin. The skyline shimmered in the atmospheric heat of a June night, a ghostly mirage under a full moon.

He'd often imagined himself here, holding hands with Amanda under the stars. He'd smoke his pipe while she recited a poem. He'd nod, pretending to understand, then she'd kiss his cheek and lead him to their bedroom.

But the dream was dead. He clutched a plastic bottle tighter, spray vanishing in the breeze. What did the amoebas think, cast upon the wind in droplets of infected spray?

Suddenly he felt the cold steel of a gun barrel pressed against the back of his neck.

"You killed her," rasped a voice.

Pugmire laughed. "Figure that out yourself, detective?"

The gun's barrel slid upward three inches.

"You murdered Roger Dubose," said Connors. "Infected him with brain-eating amoebas. Everyone knew he suffered from allergies and used nasal sprays. You cultivated amoebas in your lab, then contaminated a sprayer. What'd you use, a hypodermic needle?"

"Is this where you explain my crime? How droll."

"This is where I giftwrap you for the D.A.," said Connors. "Roger loved kayaking. Everyone would assume he'd become infected by natural means, at his lake house. It was the perfect murder. Almost."

"How'd you know Dubose didn't infect himself in the lake?"

"Roger didn't go kayaking that weekend."

Pugmire shook his head ruefully.

"I understand why you killed Roger. With him out of the way, you'd have Amanda. So why'd you kill her?"

"Because she chose you!" shouted Pugmire. "After all my years of hoping. After I'd killed for her."

The gun's hammer cocked with an audible click.

"I ought to blow your brains out."

"Come now, detective. Is that any way to treat the man who saved you from yourself?"

Pugmire felt the pressure of the barrel ease from his skull. He pictured Connors's furrowed brow, a drop of sweat running down the jut of that magnificent chin.

"What are you talking about?"

"If I hadn't killed Roger, Amanda would've convinced you to do it. She had an animal magnetism, a power. Like one of those creatures who lured sailors to their doom. What were they called?"

"Sirens," said Connors.

"Just so. I saw how your pupils dilated, how your breath quickened when you saw her. She'd bewitched your mind from the first. Did she take you to bed, Connors?"

The detective's silence was all the answer Pugmire needed.

"Eventually, you'd have killed for her. Then she'd catch your confession that you acted alone, to protect herself from prosecution."

The gun's hammer slowly clicked home. Pugmire felt a powerful grip haul him to his feet and spin him around. Connors's eyes, inches from Pugmire's, blazed with a fire deep within. If the eyes were the windows to the soul, Craig Connors was in hell.

The quiet of the night was broken by the sounds of approaching police sirens.

"It's the gurney for you," said Connors. "I'll be there, watching them inject the pentobarbital."

"You're too late." Pugmire raised the plastic spray bottle, shook it so Connors could hear the liquid inside.

Connors relaxed his grip. "You...you didn't."

"There's some left, detective. Care for a snort?"

Connors batted the bottle away and slammed a fist into Pugmire's solar plexus. The fat man grunted, doubling over. Another blow connected with his nose and he fell to his knees.

Pugmire smiled at the blood gushing down his face. Were his little friends swimming in it, flagella spinning, pseudopods questing for prey?

"Enjoy hell, Pugmire."

The microbiologist's face flushed with a feverish intensity. He felt giddy, lightheaded. Perhaps the amoebas were already working their magic. "I used to not believe in hell. But now I hope I'm wrong."

Connors scowled. "For God's sake, why?"

"Amanda will be there, waiting for me. We'll finally be together."

James A. Hearn is an attorney and author who writes in a variety of genres, including crime fiction, science fiction, fantasy, and horror. His fiction has appeared or is forthcoming in *Alfred Hitchcock's Mystery Magazine*, *The Eyes of Texas*, *Guns + Tacos*, *Monsters, Movies & Mayhem*, and *Peace, Love, and Crime*. Visit his website at JamesAHearn.com.

THE MURDER OF JONATHAN GREYSTONE

BARRY FULTON

Roland DeSilva answered a gentle knock on the door of his Fifth Avenue apartment, signaling the beginning of a high-stakes interview. Surprised by Sarah Robinson's youth and casual dress, he welcomed her with his old-world charm and suggested they meet in his study overlooking Central Park.

"Sarah," he said once they'd settled into overstuffed chairs, "I've been intrigued by your project from its inception. I trust my cooperation will allow you to put these annoying rumors to rest."

"Thanks, Mr. DeSilva, our team from the Syracuse Criminology Center has spoken to all the others, including Tony Lancaster himself. This is our final interview before wrapping up our investigation of the Greystone murder."

"A coincidence we're talking today, exactly two years after the musical opened on Broadway. The theater lost two of Broadway's finest actors with Jonathan Greystone's death and Lancaster's incarceration."

"Mr. Lancaster's attorney insists his client is innocent," Sarah said. "His friends described him as an egomaniac and generally unpleasant, but none believed him capable of murder. You knew both Greystone and Lancaster, so you may hold the key to our investigation."

"Give me a moment to get us each a coffee," DeSilva said, "and I'll tell you the story exactly as I witnessed it."

* * * *

Opening night. The overture had ended, and the curtain was going up when I rushed from backstage to take my reserved seat in the third row, center aisle. The set replicated Pittsburgh's fifty-year-old Majestic movie theater. As the lights dimmed, and the curtain in front of the movie screen parted, the classic film *Night of the Living Dead* began. It showed a 1967 Pontiac Lemans hardtop, traveling up a gentle grade on a curvy country road toward an overgrown cemetery. Johnny and Barbara stepped out of the car and walked toward their father's headstone to place a wreath.

The film stopped, and the screen disappeared to reveal a replica of an abandoned house at the edge of the cemetery. Two actors emerged from a stage version of the Pontiac. Barbara, played by Rosa Donatelli, best known for her role as Blanche DuBois in the Broadway revival of *Streetcar*. Tony Lancaster as her brother, Johnny. They turned to the audience and began singing.

> *Papa's body lies—a-mouldering in the grave,*
> *Mama still contends—he was so very brave.*
> *She took her little hatchet and plunged it in his skull,*
> *He looked at her and said, this is no fun at all.*
> *She sends us here from Pittsburgh to place a little wreath*
> *On the very gravestone that Papa's underneath.*
> *Glory, glory, hallelujah,*
> *Glory, glory, hallelujah,*
> *And his soul goes stumbling on!*

Johnny performed a soft-shoe routine followed by a solo, *Rotten in the Grave*, sung in the style of a Verdi aria. Barbara then danced and sang through the cemetery to an old jazz standard, *I'll Be Glad When You're Dead, You Rascal You*.

I'd been writing scripts since I was a kid and never heard such joyous laughter in the theater. The two actors acknowledged the applause with a bow and curtsy and exited stage left.

Modesty doesn't become me, but I must be fair. Without Tony and Rosa, the play wouldn't have enjoyed such a reception. Six-foot-two with a build that would cause your great aunt to swoon, Tony had a deep voice made for the theater and a face sculpted by God: chiseled features, angular face, aquiline nose, jutting chin, full lips, crystal-blue eyes, long eyelashes. And Rosa was dazzling, dancing across the stage in high heels, looking as if she had stepped off the cover of Diana Vreeland's 1968 *Vogue*. What skill it took to transform her from her psychotic role in *Streetcar* to the perfect companion for Tony.

Thunder, lightning, wind howling. Theater standards to set a mood. The lights dimmed as the earth rumbled. A hand rose through a trap from the stage floor. And another. Eight pairs of hands appeared, slowly followed by arms, heads, and torsos of zombies rising through the set designer's green grass.

"This is looking awfully scary," the woman seated next to me whispered to her husband. "I thought it was supposed to be a comedy."

The eight terrifying figures formed a conga line and danced among the tombstones to music drawn from Mussorgsky's *Night on Bald Mountain*. And the dancing, at first menacing, was so skillfully choreographed that the audience erupted in laughter when the eight zombies paired off and concluded with a *pas de deux*.

The zombies faded into the background as Johnny and Barbara returned to the stage. Carrying an enormous wreath, Barbara struggled under its weight to the amusement of the audience.

"Johnny," she said, "this place is spookier than ever."

"Filled with zombies, I'm sure, but don't worry, Sis, your little brother's all grown up and promises to protect you."

"Don't kid around, Johnny, I'm scared enough without your stupid zombie stories."

The earth opened up again, and another zombie bounded onto the stage and fell with a terrifying scream. Johnny backed off as it lurched toward him. It was so damn real that even I tensed. The zombie moved awkwardly across the stage, dragging one leg as Johnny continued his retreat. The theater was so quiet, I could hear the actors breathing. When another ear-splitting shriek from the zombie interrupted the silence, the woman seated to my left screamed. Comedy turned to terror. It wasn't till later that I learned the actor had unwittingly followed the classic idiom of the theater to "break a leg" by doing exactly that while being propelled from the trap room below the stage.

Billed as the star of the show, veteran actor Jonathan Greystone had described his role playing a terrifying zombie as the culmination of a distinguished career.

"I've done it all," he told *Playbill*. "Twice nominated for an Academy Award, once for playing George Bernard Shaw and a second time for Babe Ruth. Curiously, I consider this role as the capstone of my career."

His makeup rendered him unrecognizable. But who else had the skill to evoke a palpable feeling of evil within minutes of appearing on stage?

When the curtain came down at the end of Act One, the audience remained silent, frozen in terror for what seemed forever. But eight or ten seconds later they burst into sustained applause.

* * * *

I stood alone in the lobby wearing a smile to disguise my growing discomfort. Compliments all around me for the cast, not a word about the playwright. And those who weren't sharing their delight were busy on the cell phones tweeting about the stars.

The *Times* critic eventually spotted me.

"This is your baby, isn't it?" he said.

"You're not sure?"

"Yeah, but Greystone owns the night. Zombies everywhere these days, but he's unique. Feels like a Mel Brooks script."

"Thanks," I said, repressing my anger at being assigned a copycat role by the only person who actually recognized me.

* * * *

Back in my seat as the curtain opened for Act Two. The scene began inside the abandoned home with Johnny and Barbara watching a thirteen-inch black and white TV. The announcer reported that "zombies are eating the flesh of the people they kill."

"Johnny, they're coming for us. I can see them moving toward the house."

"Good lord, Barbara, we're dinner if we don't run."

They embraced and sang in the style of Jeanette MacDonald and Nelson Eddy.

> *This is no fun. It's time to run.*
> *It has no appeal, to be someone's meal.*
> *They're getting close, we'll soon be toast.*
> *We need a diversion, a little excursion.*
> *We'll run for the car, it can't be far.*
> *If it's not too late, to avoid a culinary fate.*

They sang with such vaudevillian esprit that I joined the audience in extended laughter.

I ignored the man seated behind me when he whispered to his wife, "silly lyrics."

More singing and dancing continued until the grand finale.

> *We'd like to live, but haven't the will,*
> *Our lives are worthless atop this hill.*
> *But all's not lost, we can dance and sing*
> *Even in death we could have a fling.*
> *Our lips stammer, what shall we do?*
> *Here we are, without a clue.*
> *What does the afterlife as a zombie bring?*
> *Oh death, where is thy sting-a-ling-a-ling?*

The zombies encircled Johnny and Barbara as they concluded, lifted their hands and looked upward, all chanting in Latin "*et sepulcrum tuum victoria.*"

* * * *

Curtain calls when it ended? I lost count.

I hurried backstage to congratulate the director, a friend of many years. A scowling man in uniform stopped me.

"Where're you heading, Mister?"

"Back stage, if you don't mind."

Flashing a police badge, he said, "Not a chance. It's a crime scene."

"Too bad, but I'm the playwright. I wrote the book *and* the lyrics."

"I don't care if you wrote the Holy Bible. One more word outta you, and I'm placing you under arrest."

* * * *

The next morning's *Times* explained the police presence under the headline: TRAGEDY TERRORIZES THEATER.

> Legendary actor Jonathan Greystone disappeared an hour before curtain time at the opening of "Night of the Lively Dead." The police were called when a stagehand found a pool of blood in his dressing room. No body has yet been found. Nonetheless, the production was hailed by our critic as "spectacular, haunting, and hilarious." An unknown understudy who substituted for Greystone ran away with the show, upstaging heartthrob Tony Lancaster. Playing the role of a terrifying zombie, the actor literally broke a leg while arriving on stage and performed throughout the performance in excruciating pain.

The theater went dark the next day as the police continued their investigation.

Ticket sales soared, and I returned to my seat in the third row when it reopened a day later. Before the curtain went up, the audience buzzed with rumors that Greystone had been murdered. The late edition of the *Daily News* reported Tony Lancaster had been taken into custody. I overheard a woman insisting that Rosa Donatelli was the murderer.

"My brother's a cop," she said, "and he told me they're sure Rosa did it. It's all hush-hush now, but she'll be arrested as soon as they get a *habeas corpus* or something from a judge."

Rosa had threatened to kill Greystone during rehearsal if he ever again put his ghoulish hands on her behind, although I'm sure she didn't mean it literally. The director foolishly told the cops it might have been the understudy. Not a shred of evidence, of course, but enough to ruin a career.

As the lights went down, the audience eyed each of the actors with giddy suspicion. Tony Lancaster's appearance ended one rumor. He had not been taken into police custody. And who could believe that a woman with the innocent face of Rosa Donatelli could commit murder?

The unknown understudy, a woman now fully credited in the program as Virginia Lugosi, appeared with her leg in a cast and remained hauntingly ghoulish. Her awkward movements and torturous groaning probably did not come solely from some latent talent but at least in part from the pain of a fracture. The amateur sleuths in the audience must have realized there hadn't been time for her to kill Greystone, hide the body, and get in costume with full makeup.

* * * *

"Mr. DeSilva, sorry to interrupt," Sarah said, doing just that to the tale I was relating. "Did you suspect Tony at that time?"

"I'm a playwright, not a detective. I chose not to add to the rumors." He cleared his throat. "To continue…"

* * * *

The first act ended with more applause than opening night. The comedic terror on stage had been heightened by Greystone's disappearance. During intermission, when I stood alone in the lobby, a reporter approached me.

"You must know a few things," he said. "Has the missing body been found?"

"Not a clue, and if the cops know, they aren't talking."

"I've been working on the story all day, and they won't share anything."

"Maybe they're also baffled," I said.

"Yeah, maybe, but I have a theory that explains everything. There has been no murder. The so-called understudy is actually Greystone himself. It's all a publicity stunt. Take off that makeup and remove that phony plaster cast, and you'll find Greystone."

I snorted.

The house lights flashed to signal that Act Two was about to begin. When Tony and Rosa sang their duet with the zombies closing in, the two looked as though a murderer still lurked in the wings waiting for more victims. The lyrics fit the occasion. The hint of real danger elicited cautious laugher. The killer was still at large.

Tony Lancaster and Rosa Donatelli had seldom performed with such energy. And the new sensation, Virginia Lugosi, must have been the scariest zombie ever to appear on stage. This unknown transgender woman had neatly upstaged two of Broadway's favorites.

Immediately after the third curtain call, I spotted Virginia with two uniformed cops. Her head down, she hobbled past me on crutches. She had been arrested. She looked up at me, forced a smile, and said, "Looks like I got my fifteen minutes of fame."

* * * *

The following morning, she was pictured on the front page of the *New York Post* being escorted out of the theater between the two cops. How did the photographer get the shot? At least she was shown on crutches. Otherwise a picture of her in handcuffs would have been tantamount to guilt.

Without her, the show practically fell apart the next night. Tony and Rosa were lackluster. An anonymous source from the NYPD had told a reporter that Virginia's fingerprints were found on a bloody knife in Greystone's dressing room.

After two more evenings of listless performances and disgruntled patrons, Virginia's agent, Mark Zabinsky, confessed to the crime. "I had no choice," he said, "after Greystone's threats."

Virginia was released when Zabinsky told the police the sordid story that began on the first day of rehearsal.

* * * *

"How did you learn this, Mr. DeSilva?" Sarah asked.

"A buddy in the police department shared the transcript. I'll read you a few excerpts that reveal his eagerness to sacrifice his freedom for hers."

* * * *

"She had been flattered when Greystone offered to mentor her," Zabinsky told the detective. "Her first time in a Broadway play, even as an understudy, was the culmination of years of training and failed tryouts. By the third week of rehearsal, Graystone's courtly attention had become more familiar. Greetings with an air kiss had evolved to greater intimacy. Gentle goodnight hugs were held longer. She had accepted his attention as signs of an evolving friendship until the night he insisted she join him for a nightcap. She agreed, assuming they were going to his club. She should have objected when they stepped out of a cab and were greeted by the doorman of an apartment building at Gramercy Park.

"They were barely inside his apartment," Zabinsky said, "before he grabbed her, kissed her, and promised to make her a star. At first politely and then forcefully, she rejected his advances. He had no idea this tall statuesque woman held a first *dan* blackbelt in judo. As she headed toward the door, he cursed her and promised to ruin her career if she left his apartment. She rushed out, called me, and we returned to our walk-up apartment in SoHo. As you must have guessed, our relationship grew deeper than client-agent.

"What she had previously perceived as friendly banter at rehearsals became non-stop harassment with vile threats and ugly gestures. When Greystone said he had described her to *Variety* as a transvestite crack whore, she considered quitting the show. She still lacked confidence in her recent transition as a trans woman. I persuaded her to stay, promised that Greystone would never have the opportunity to damage her career."

Greystone's missing body was found on a catwalk three stories above the stage within a few feet of the freight elevator. Not by the police, who had never looked up, but by a guy from the lighting crew who had climbed up to adjust several spotlights. So much for the reporter calling it a publicity stunt. Greystone was stone-cold dead.

At Zabinsky's insistence, Virginia returned to the stage.

Despite the early rumors, I believe everyone had ruled out Rosa. In a long career, more than a few actors had undoubtedly tried to take advantage of her, and she hadn't killed them. She could take care of herself without wielding a knife.

Tony, however, had the look of a man benumbed with guilt. Maybe a writer's imagination—maybe intuition.

* * * *

Later, the homicide detective told me he had asked Tony to come by the precinct station the next morning. Perfect in every way, he arrived wearing a tailored blazer over three-hundred dollar jeans, a frayed hot pink shirt, and a Dolce and Gabanna turquoise bow tie.

I learned from a friend in the department that the detective had done his homework. First complimented Tony on his acting career and then asked if he and Greystone had been lovers. "That's ridiculous," Tony said. "I didn't come here to be slandered."

"Just a question," the detective said. "Is it true that Greystone has sued you for alienation of affection?"

Tony exploded in mock indignation, stood up, and asked if he was free to leave. The detective answered in the affirmative. "Of course, you're not charged with a crime—not yet! Before you go, you may wish to glance at these pictures we found in Greystone's apartment. They would suggest you two may have been *very* close friends."

Tony had friends? What a surprise. He could have played Narcissus without a script. Once during rehearsal, I complimented him on his performance. He nodded, barely acknowledged me, and walked away. Probably looking for a mirror. Here's the guy who's getting all the attention for mouthing my words, *my* words. And he doesn't even remember me. The stupid bastard is applauded for memorizing a script that took me a year to write. And he barely recognizes me.

Tony returned to the theater after leaving the police station. In his previous performances, he had fought furiously for his life and died with an anguished cry. That night, he barely resisted and died peacefully.

As fans recall from the movie, the recent dead immediately return as zombies. My script embraced that trope as Johnny himself rose from the dead. More zombie-like than the other actors, he staggered and stomped toward the abandoned home where his distraught sister hid in fear.

In my version of the story, Barbara thinks Johnny is still alive and rushes from the house to greet him. She embraces him but immediately sees the pallor of his skin and recognizes the stench of death. She tries to pull away, but he holds her and begins to sing in a plaintive voice.

Mama's waitin' in Pittsburgh, Pennsylvania,

For our return, from this wicked zombie mania.
Still on Squirrel Hill, where we were born and bred,
I wonder if she'll care when she learns we're both dead.

When he begins to gnaw on her arm, Barbara escapes from his clutches and dashes to the front of the stage, imploring the audience for help in a full-throated solo.

Please tell Johnny I have a tough hide,
All sinew and bone with offal inside.
Low in protein, high in fat
Fewer nutrients than a Norway rat.

Johnny slowly creeps forward and tenderly puts his arm around Barbara. She looks up and smiles. They conclude with a duet, alternating verses as the eight dancing zombies perform a minuet.

"Oh, Johnny," she begins, *"I've grown accustomed to your smell,"*
"Barbara," he responds, *"are you sure you're feeling well?"*
"If only you'll recall...culinary incest's against the law."
"But, Sis, you'd be so tasty, a piece of leg, a little titty."
"A scandalous thought me thinks, and not so very witty."

The earth rumbled, and the lead zombie returned to the stage. Virginia Lugosi was back, determined to be remembered for what she feared might be her final performance. She extended her hand to Barbara, who pulled her to her feet. Then she surprised everyone, including me, by turning to Johnny and singing words I had not written in a voice that still haunts me.

I see murder in your eyes
Beneath your sad disguise.
You killed Greystone, I know,
And I'll never let it go
Until you rot for good
As you damn well know you should.

The curtain came down. Thunderous applause. Standing ovations. Tony Lancaster did not appear for the curtain call. I hesitated to go backstage, cautious not to be close to Tony in a fit of rage. Virginia would undoubtedly be dismissed but never forgotten.

The homicide detective spotted me in the lobby, asked if I would answer a few questions. I agreed and confirmed I did not write the concluding number. He suggested we find a quiet place to talk. We took a booth at the Backstage Bistro two doors away, so noisy we could not be overheard.

"Understand you've been at rehearsals and nearly every performance," he said. "What do you know?"

Unprepared for that, I paused while we ordered drinks. Then I replied, "What do I know? Only what I read—and what I see. Nothing more."

"Hmm," he mused. "Her agent, Mark Zabinsky, confessed to the crime, as you are no doubt aware. He's in custody, swears he did it, and doesn't want a lawyer. However, Tony Lancaster remains a person of interest. So, tell me, what have you *seen* that might help me unravel the murder?"

"I barely know Zabinsky, but if he's confessed, doesn't that wrap it up?"

The cop shook his head. "Not if he was seen by two witnesses at Madison Square Garden watching some Mexican bruiser become the World Heavyweight Champion at the moment of the murder. He may be charged with interfering in an official investigation. We're gonna release his sorry ass in the morning. Confessed to protect his client, his androgynous girlfriend, the zombie who once was a boy—if I have that straight."

"Yeah, Virginia Lugosi, which as you probably discovered isn't her real name. For an actor, it's far more memorable than Virginia Butler."

"How about Tony? What have you seen? Does *he* have a motive?"

"If jealousy is a motive, yes," I said. "But that would put practically every actor not chosen for the lead under suspicion. Everyone in the cast knows he resented the attention Greystone received before the play opened."

I was being circumspect with the detective, careful not to convey my pleasure in Greystone's death. He had been abusing aspiring actresses for years, promising them fame for sex. Did he know Virginia was a trans-woman when he tried to seduce her, attempted to rape her?

I suggested he speak again with Tony's leading lady, Rosa Donatelli. I still remember what she told me of her cursory exchange with the detective.

"I can't imagine Tony as a murderer," she told him. "He could be difficult, demanding, and even abusive, but not as bad as Greystone. His arrogance was a sign of his insecurity, of a man uncertain of his identity and sexuality."

"You two friends?" the detective then asked her.

"Professionally, yes, but not socially."

"Anything else?"

"Well, yes," she replied. "Does Virginia's release mean she's no longer a suspect?"

Rosa told me he didn't reply.

The police asked Virginia to return to the station. Obviously, I wasn't present during her interrogation, but I can imagine the scene. She nervously answers questions she'd heard before when a police officer enters the room with a small box and hands a pair of latex gloves to the detective. He puts on the gloves, opens the box, and removes a knife.

"Have you ever seen this?" he asks.

"It looks like the prop I use in the play," she answers.

"Look closely," he says. "Is it yours?"

"No, I don't think so. The blade looks real. I mean, mine looks real, too, but it's made of plastic. Actors don't go on stage with real knives."

I imagine the detective taps the knife on the table to confirm it's real, not a prop, and points to the blood stains on the blade. She shudders and asks if it's the knife that killed Greystone, and then repeats her denial that it wasn't hers, that she didn't kill anyone. And through tears, she says, "I can't deny I had a motive, but I didn't kill that lecherous bastard." The interview concludes when Virginia is unable to answer how her fingerprints were found on the handle of the knife.

* * * *

"Mr. DeSilva, your story is fascinating," Sarah said, "but if she couldn't explain the fingerprints, why didn't the police charge her?"

"Well, Sarah, they screwed up when they first arrested her. I'd guess they'd decided not to risk it again until they had more evidence."

* * * *

The show went on while the investigation continued. A new rumor practically every day. There wasn't a member of the cast or crew that someone didn't suspect. The director? Conductor? Bassoon player? Even me?

Finally, the detective found evidence compelling enough to make an arrest: a charge of eighty-five dollars from Toledo Forge on Tony Lancaster's Amex card. It explained the fingerprints on the knife and definitely cleared Virginia.

* * * *

The prosecuting attorney's performance at Tony's trial was compelling theater.

"Ladies and gentleman of the jury," he began. "You have seen the evidence, the bloody knife thrust into the heart of Jonathan Greystone. And you were told the knife carried the fingerprints of a struggling young actress. You were shown a picture of her fingerprints on a six-foot-wide screen and asked to imagine Greystone's stunned disbelief an hour before the opening performance when Virginia allegedly struck with the knife.

"Allow me to remind you of the picture I presented: a schematic diagram of the knife showing the metal blade extending through the handle. To be precise, I identified the *tang* to which the *scales* were riveted. The *scales,* made of a resin composite, are attached after the knife is forged to provide a comfortable grip. Her fingerprints were on the *scales*, not on the metal that pierced his heart. Furthermore, the *scales* found on the real knife had been removed from the plastic prop used in the theater, used by Virginia during rehearsal, used by Virginia rehearsing as Greystone's understudy. She was being framed, as I will show you.

"Tony Lancaster ordered a real knife from Toledo Forge in Brooklyn, sent to him at the theater and charged to his credit card. He switched the *scales* from her prop knife with her fingerprints, joined Greystone in his dressing room, killed him an hour before the opening, dragged his body to the freight elevator, and left it on the catwalk three stories above the stage.

"Motive? To silence Greystone about their homosexual affair and to prevent him from receiving the acclaim that Tony Lancaster believed was his due."

The jury found Tony guilty of murder. The play continued without him. His attorney appealed. The conviction was upheld. After two years in prison, he's now eligible for parole in eighteen more years.

* * * *

"So, Mr. DeSilva, you're convinced that justice was done?" Sarah asked.

"Without a doubt, as the jury concluded. His attorney's constant bleating that Tony was incapable of murder is balderdash. We're all capable, aren't we? Although few of us ever cross to the dark side."

"Thank you, Mr. DeSilva. Your insights will help our team to a conclusion. Thanks for your time—and congratulations on the continuing success of your musical. I understand it recently opened in London to rave reviews."

* * * *

Now retired from writing, I've reached my Biblical promise of three score and ten years. Sarah's criminology team eventually concluded that Tony Lancaster had been rightly convicted. *Night of the Lively Dead* is still playing in the Marquis Theater, soon to hit its fifth anniversary.

I'm enjoying my twilight years in Sicily on the eastern side of the island within a few steps of the sea. I'm at peace here, where no one knows my name, mourns the death of Jonathan Greystone, or cares about Tony Lancaster's conviction. Virginia had no idea of my scheme to ensure she was charged and then released. She sends me an occasional postcard in appreciation of my support.

The talent I first spotted in Virginia has taken her to even greater acclaim. She was exciting as a zombie on stage, but her notoriety as the accused murderer launched her career with the public. She was recently nominated for an Academy Award for her role in a remake of *Anatomy of a Murder* co-starring Daniel Day-Lewis.

Tony would be free today, still on stage, if he had used the only credible defense that would have saved him: that he was too damn dumb to have conceived of and executed such a complex crime. The fool told his attorney he didn't know how his credit card was used at Toledo Forge. Anyone could have "borrowed" it from his dressing room and returned it the following day. Poor Tony is paying a steep price for his outsized ego while I'm enjoying a quiet life in *Siracusa*.

I've prepared a sealed envelope for my executor with my script for the perfect crime. On my death it will confirm my brilliance as a playwright and afford me the credit I've long deserved. When my adaption of that tawdry movie is long forgotten, I'll always be remembered for *The Murder of Jonathan Greystone*.

✗

Barry Fulton writes the Thomas Sebastian Scott Espionage/Mystery series: *The Irish Imbroglio, Behind the Seventh Veil, The Lady is Bugged*, and *Flame: Hackers, Artists, Lovers, and Spies*. He is a member of the Washington Institute of Foreign Affairs, Public Diplomacy Council, DACOR, and former board member of the Salzburg Global Seminar. A retired diplomat, Air Force officer, and university professor, he has been posted to NATO, Italy, Japan, Pakistan, and Turkey.

YOU GOTTA BE IN IT!

ELLIOTT CAPON

With a population of almost three hundred thousand, our township is more populous than many American cities. We're big enough to have three zip codes. I was the Tuesday-to-Saturday desk clerk at the smallest of the three post offices in the township. I'm told that years ago you'd have a line going out the door, especially on Saturdays. But nowadays, with more and more people paying their bills online, the demand for stamps is way down. Sure, we get a little busy around Easter and Valentine's Day, and of course Christmas and Chanukah, but for the most part the stamp business is slow. People will come in and buy a book of twenty stamps, and that covers their birthday and anniversary cards for a year.

We do have our regulars, of course. People who can't or won't pay bills online, people with small home businesses who ship packages with some regularity, people who use our money orders as their checking accounts. And in the nine years I've been working at this relatively small post office, I've gotten to know many of the regulars, at least for pleasant chat purposes. Funny, though, that I don't know any of them by name: I know them by their addresses.

So this one day, a Wednesday, as I recall, in comes 1811 Thirty-Fourth Street, a guy in his mid-sixties who generally buys fifty stamps a month, and shows up once or twice a week with padded envelopes. He says he's eking out a hobby by selling articles and stories and the occasional novel to low-paying markets, that's why he's always mailing manuscripts. Me, I don't know. I would think that, concurrent with the demise of the stamp, the era of the printed manuscript with the self-addressed stamped envelope for the manuscript's return had gone the way of the dodo. I suspect that our little post office is complicit in the transportation of goods that the police generally frown upon, but, hey, I'm not the postal police, I'm a clerk.

But anyway, I've known 1811 Thirty-Fourth Street for eight years now, and since there's rarely anyone else in the place when he comes in, we usually chat about the weather, the new school budget with the concordant higher property taxes, and so on. As I said, he's in his mid-sixties, which makes him about ten years older than me; we're practically peers.

So anyway on this Wednesday, he comes in and asks for a Priority Mail Express envelope. I point out to him where we keep them, by the table behind him, and ask him just to fill out the form and then let me have it—I'll attach it for him. It takes him a minute or so to fill out the form, and I can see he put a #10 envelope into the red, white, and blue envelope and sealed it shut. Then he brought it back to the counter.

I saw that he had addressed the label to the State Lottery Commission. I was surprised.

"What's this?" I asked. I knew him; I could ask something like that.

Guy looked fit to burst. "I won the Win-6, two weeks ago!" he said, and for the first time in my life I heard someone actually *crow*, like you'll read in fiction. "The January sixth drawing, I had the only winning ticket. Two and a half million dollars!" I'd never seen someone so just, literally, exploding with joy.

"That's wonderful!" I declared, because, after all, he was an acquaintance and I was happy for him. But no one is allowed that kind of joy without having their chops busted a little. "You know," I said thoughtfully, "you're only going to net about sixty percent of that. That's about…uh…"—quick calculation—"…about a million and a half you walk away with."

He knew I was having fun with him, so he put on a sad face and said, "Yeah, well it'll have to do." We both paused, then burst into laughter. After the laughter petered out, I said, "Why'd you wait till now?"

Boy, I thought he was going to hand out cigars as he explained to me. He'd watched the live January 6 drawing on the locallest of the local TV stations, and realized he had all six numbers. He checked the State Lottery website an hour later and saw that his was indeed the only winning ticket: $2,508,444. He put the ticket in the kitchen cookie jar, and thought it best to keep his mouth shut and then file the claim form (available online) in a month or two…but he couldn't wait. So here he was, in my post office, on January 15, with the ticket and the claim form ready to go to arrive at the state capitol the next day. Without my having to ask, he pointed out that he had a dozen photocopies of the ticket and the claim form stashed in hidey-holes all over the house and even his safe deposit box.

Keeping it jocular, I asked him what he was going to say at the press conference. He pointed out to me, which I'd never bothered to think about, that in this era of Powerballs and Megamillionses in the hundreds of millions of dollars, someone winning one of fifty state lotteries for a "lousy" three-four-five million dollars was no longer news. *Maybe* the local neighborhood paper would report on a win like that, but there were almost never any press conferences or six o'clock news appearances for the state's (any state's) five thousandth millionaire.

So anyway, I took his fifteen dollars for postage, congratulated him again, and flipped the cardboard envelope into the large (but mostly empty) canvas outgoing cart that stood behind me. He left, and I swear that his feet didn't touch the ground on his way out.

I hate Edgar Allen Poe. He's the one who introduced me, years ago, to the concept of "The Imp of the Perverse," that nagging *something* in your brain that makes you do things you *absolutely KNOW* are wrong or dangerous.

Alone in the small lobby, I happened to glance over at the big-wheeled canvas tub and saw a corner of a red, white, and blue cardboard envelope. There was a winning lottery ticket in there. A ticket worth, after taxes, about a million and a half dollars.

I didn't have a gambling problem. I had a *losing* problem. Nobody was threatening to break my legs…yet…but a lot of my late mother's jewelry and silver and my late father's stamp and coin collections were enjoying their new home at Fairview Loans and Pawnbrokers, and there wasn't much left to surrender to them. My debtors loved to see me enter their establishments. I heard one of them appreciatively joke in a voice that was not quite low enough that I could lose a hand even if I held a royal flush and everyone else had folded. But I knew the welcome would wear out as soon as I couldn't cover the week's interest (forget the principal!).

A million and a half would go a long way. It would erase my debt. It would let me relocate to another state, get a fresh start—yeah, maybe keep continuing to work for the post office. The pay was adequate and the benefits more than fair, but to *not be* in the jurisdiction of my genial casino host Mr. Masnadiero would be a really good thing. A million and a half would go a *long, long* way. And there it was, almost literally cash, sitting right there…

I had to reject the first impulse: just grab the envelope, tear it open, pocket the ticket, shred the envelope, and then wait three months or so and claim the prize (you had a year). Because within a few days, 1811 Thirty-Fourth Street would contact the Lottery people and ask where his check was. And they'd say, "We never got your claim form." And then he'd go online and track his priority mail receipt, which of course I had scanned *irretrievably* into the computer when I registered it, and there'd be no doubt that this guy with photocopies of the winning ticket and proof that he'd addressed a priority envelope to the Lottery Commission was the rightful owner of my one point five million, and there would go that. *Plus,* some detective from the postal police would wonder how a Priority envelope had somehow disappeared between the counter where I was working and the tub an arm's length from me.

No, that envelope just couldn't disappear; it had to disappear…*spectacularly.*

Customers rarely visited during the week, so I often spent hours alone at the counter, and I had time to think. 1811 Thirty-Fourth Street had come in about nine-thirty. I always locked the front door at four-thirty. Manny Alvarado would show up usually around a quarter to five, with the large van the post office subcontracted to run around to various suburban post offices, pick up the mail, and take it to the county's central distribution center.

How could that envelope disappear so that everyone was *content* that it had disappeared? Five after eleven. *Bang.* Imp of the Perverse.

It was destroyed in the fire.

What fire? Was I really going to—did I have the testosterone, the nerve to—no no no no no no no. First of all, Maggie worked in the back, doing the sorting and taking over the counter when I went to the bathroom or to lunch. We had four carriers who were in and out all day. I was absolutely not going to risk the lives of my co-workers. Also, we were attached on one side to a laundromat and on the other to a dog-grooming salon. I wasn't going to put innocent people at risk. Plus the fact that post offices in the suburbs rarely burn down, not being known for housing tanks of propane or active volcanoes. So not only would the postal police be in on this, the county prosecutor doubtless had at least one arson investigator on the payroll.

When life hands you lemons, *et al*. There couldn't be a fire right here in the building, but…it was not unknown for motor vehicles to burst into flame.

Quarter after eleven. Manny'd be here in about four and a half hours.

I got my smartphone out and went on the internet.

Yes, you can get hints right there. I won't tell you where. I *won't*. It's not lack of knowledge that keeps us free from most crime, but the fear of getting caught that deters would-be felons. By a quarter to twelve, I had that million and a half in my hands, I was living in a brand-new state, and I was breathing easy for the first time in years. At lunchtime, I visited two different hardware stores and bought mineral spirits and candles. I ran into the dollar store and bought plastic cups and disposable exam gloves. Then I stopped by the house, took some gasoline out of the lawnmower, and poured it into an empty pickle jar that I keep for bacon grease.

Three minutes after I returned from lunch, there was no Priority Mail envelope in my canvas bin, no claim form with 1811 Thirty-Fourth Street's name on it. There was a lottery ticket dated January 6th in my wallet: five games, the fourth one with each number underlined.

Did I feel bad for 1811 Thirty-Fourth Street, for Manny? Sure I did. A little. But the history of humankind, going back to the Australopithecines and the Homo Habilises and the Ramapithicuses is: you snooze you lose. Might makes right. Possession is nine-tenths of the law. I wasn't actually stealing from 1811 Thirty-Fourth Street—it wasn't his money to begin with, he'd *won* it: I wasn't taking anything *away* from him. And Manny? He just worked for the company, he didn't own the van. I was sure he'd get away without being hurt—the fire would be contained to the rear of the van, anyway. The past year alone, I've seen news reports of a dozen burning cars on the highway, with people always being pulled out safely.

Speaking of Poe again, remember the narrator of "The Tell-Tale Heart"? Remember how he bragged about how calm he was, how gracious he behaved to the detectives when they first showed up? Yeah, well, I know. That was me the rest of the day. I wouldn't have been more relaxed, more pleasant with the few customers I had in the afternoon, more helpful to Maggie. It was like I'd taken a proverbial chill pill. I felt like I had swallowed one of those euphoric drugs they sell at clubs and schoolyards.

Bingo, four-thirty. Maggie went home and I locked the front door. Four thirty-five, and my last carrier dropped off his truck and we wished each other a good night.

Four-forty-seven, Manny pulled down the driveway and backed up to the loading dock. *Manny,* I said, paraphrasing myself, *we don't have much today. Listen, I got some bagels in the kitchenette. Go get yourself one, I can load this myself. Yeah, yeah, yeah, I'm sure. There's coffee, too. I know you don't get home till after eight, eat a little something. G'head, g'head, I ain't that old that I can't throw a few sacks into the back of a van!*

Again, no details. A chimpanzee wearing Coke-bottle-bottom glasses could, with a few clicks of a mouse, figure out how to set up the—uh, shall we say contraption or device or system that I hid in the back of the van. I slammed the door shut, and a grateful Manny, with a teeny bit of cream cheese on his chin, thanked me, said he'd see me the next day, and took off for his next stop.

Didn't even make the six o'clock news. The next day, in the local newspaper's website, if you clicked on "Township News," you would find a little paragraph about a mail van mysteriously catching fire. No one was hurt (*whew,* I went) but whatever mail had been in the back of the truck—he'd made three stops—had been burnt to cinders.

1811 Thirty-Fourth Street came back in with another thick envelope on the twenty-fourth. He looked glum, which is the first time in my life I've ever used that word.

"Whassamatta?" I asked.

"Remember that lottery ticket?"

"The winner?"

He nodded, and now his glumness turn to a wry, sour smile. "I think it was in that van that burned up."

I'd been practicing in front of the mirror. "Oh, no!" I declared with horror.

"Yeah." He allowed himself a one-chuck chuckle. "Even though I had the copies, lottery rules are you need the original. No original, no prize."

"Oh!" I commiserated. "That sucks."

He gestured. "Easy come, easy go. The Lord giveth and the Lord taketh away. It is better to have loved and lost, *et cetera*. Spilled milk, y'know? In any case, let's get this here in the mail."

I charged him an ounce less than the package actually weighed, and let him know. It was the least I could do.

I decided that April 15 would be the day I presented my winning ticket to the Lottery offices, because that was a good ironic date, and I was in a very upbeat mood.

CLIP FROM WAPB NEWS AT SIX, APRIL 15

FEMALE ANCHOR

And now, for today's "Crime Doesn't Pay" segment, we go live to Patricia Havens in front of the Jay County Courthouse, in Mountainside.

CUT TO REPORTER IN FRONT OF COURTHOUSE

REPORTER

Yes, Katie, I'm here in front of the county courthouse where, an hour ago, U.S. Post Office worker Jack Samuelson was arraigned on charges of attempting to cash in a counterfeit Win-6 Lottery ticket.

INSERT VIDEO OF A MAN IN HIS FIFTIES, WEARING A USPS UNIFORM AND HANDCUFFS, BEING ESCORTED OUT OF COURTHOUSE

REPORTER (CONT'D)

Apparently Mr. Samuelson presented a lottery ticket from the January 6 drawing, with the winning numbers, and demanded payment. Unfortunately for him, the winning ticket had already been claimed by someone else on January 21. His ticket was deemed to be counterfeit, and he was arrested right there on the spot.

CUT TO SPLIT SCREEN: REPORTER/ANCHOR

ANCHOR

How did they know it was counterfeit?

REPORTER

Well first, Katie, the serial number on the ticket, which did indeed have the winning Win-6 numbers, was wrong. Each printed lottery ticket gets a unique serial number as it's printed, and the Lottery's computers of course keep track of that. *And* the fact that somebody else had already claimed and collected the prize.

ANCHOR (unable to contain her amusement)

How did the, uh, suspect not know that that particular jackpot had already been claimed?

REPORTER (also trying not to chortle)

Katie, lottery winnings in the two to five million dollar range are no longer big news. You have to look up the results online to see if anybody won the last drawing. You won't see that on the local news. Crime, again, apparently, does not pay. Patricia Havens, WAPB News.

END SPLIT SCREEN—CUT TO ANCHOR

ANCHOR

Let that be a lesson to all you would-be con artists out there. [She turns her head and laughs] I'm sorry. But…this is one *dumb* criminal.

At that moment, a man in his mid-sixties, residing at 1811 Thirty-Fourth Street, got down on his knees in front of his TV, looked up at the ceiling, and thanked God. Then he went down to the basement and dismantled his little printing press.

✗

Elliott Capon is the author of four published novels: *The Prince of Horror*; the comic semi-sequels of Poverty-Row Hollywood, *The Corps Vanishes* and *Meanwhile, Back at the Ranch;* and the black-comedy murder mystery *Authors' Rep*. There's also the punny collection *Damn The Torn Speedos! Full Speed Ahead!: 101 Shaggy Dogs*. There are also innumerable short stories and several reprints, all of which, to the best of our knowledge, are still sitting on someone's desk at the Pulitzer Committee offices.

THE YOU-DON'T-KNOW-THE-HALF-OF-IT-DEARIE BLUES

MICHAEL KURLAND

AN ALEXANDER BRASS MYSTERY

We had been kicked out of our offices in the *New York World* building yesterday morning, and were setting up shop in Brass's Fifth Avenue apartment, Brass, Gloria and I. Now and into the indefinite future Alexander Brass and his entourage were *persona* goddamn *non grata* at the *New York World*, the *New York World* Syndicate, and all the real estate, offices, warehouses, storehouses, way stations, assignees of value and of no value, possessions, colonies, satrapies, fiefs, vehicles both moving and stationary, motor driven and horse drawn, of which the aforementioned newspaper and publishing syndicate might be possessed or may from time to time acquire. This included most especially the suite of offices on the seventeenth floor of the *New York World* building on Fifty-Ninth Street and Tenth Avenue, Manhattan, from which for a decade until the day before yesterday Brass had produced his syndicated daily column, "Brass Tacks."

Winston Sanders, publisher of the *World* and owner of the *World* Syndicate, was mightily displeased with Alexander Brass, columnist, critic, social gadfly, pedant and my boss. Those were his words: "mightily displeased." Their relationship went back to 1921, when Brass had moved over to the *World* from doing second-string theater reviews at the *New York Herald*. For the past fifteen years they had agreed on almost nothing of any importance: Sanders was an Episcopalian, Brass an agnostic; Sanders was a Republican, Brass a Monarchist; Sanders thought Roosevelt should be impeached, F.D.R. was one of Brass's three candidates for monarch; Sanders thought that Freedom of Speech meant freedom for the publisher to have absolute control over everything that goes into his newspaper, Brass thought that altering one word of his prose was an assault on American Democracy, Motherhood and Apple Pie. Despite this they had managed a decade and a half of co-existence with a facade of mutual respect and toleration. Until two days ago.

But the roots of the dispute go back about two months, to a Thursday in December 1935. At three o'clock that afternoon Mrs. Lucy Berlinder took the train into the City from her home in Valhalla, New York, arriving at Grand Central at three forty, and at the apartment of her daughter, Mrs. Helen Weld, on Seventy-Fourth just off Central Park West, at quarter past four. She was bringing a dress she had altered for her daughter and a golden cake with chocolate icing that she had made for her nine-year-old grandson Billy, who had a heart condition and was kept home from school, so she expected to find him there.

When the elevator man let her out on the fourth floor, she rang the door-bell and knocked. And rang the doorbell and knocked. After waiting what seemed to her to be at least half an hour and getting no response, and, fearing she didn't know what, she fished the spare key her daughter had given her from her purse and opened the door. She yelled *"Helen!—Billy!"* There was no answer. Her heart, she said later, went into her throat. She went through into the living room and then the kitchen. There was a plate on the table with the crusts of a sandwich, and an empty glass of milk in the sink. She retraced her steps and went to the master bedroom. The door was closed. For a long moment she stared at the door, trying not to think—anything. She opened the door. Her daughter was sprawled half on and half off the bed in a white silk negligee with a great pool of blood under and around her and, according to the medical examiner, three shallow slashes in her neck and upper chest and one deep cut in the neck that, it turned out, had severed her carotid artery. In another bedroom she found Billy—her grandson—lying on his bed fully dressed. His arms were at his side and his legs were together, and he was dead. There were no obvious wounds. He looked, she said, like one of his toy soldiers, rigid and stiff.

Mrs. Berlinder staggered out of the apartment into the hallway and was throwing up in a waste can when the elevator man arrived in answer to her ring. The doorman called the police, who arrived within ten minutes, and the homicide detectives within twenty. The investigation came up with a series of negatives: there were no signs of foul play on Billy's body (it was later established that he had been smothered, probably in his sleep, with a pillow that was found stuffed into a clothes hamper in the bathroom), there was no murder weapon in the apartment, there was no one who wished Helen Weld harm. The most likely scenario was that someone had come up behind Helen, grabbed her under the chin, and slashed her throat. But there was no clue of who this might be. There was a knife missing from a set in the kitchen, but whether it was the one used it was impossible to tell. The elevator man had taken no one but Mrs. Berlinder up to the apartment since Dr. Steven Weld, the victim's husband, left for his office at 8:30 that morning, the back door was locked but not bolted from the inside, and Helen had definitely been alive after her husband left since several people including her mother had spoken to her on the phone.

The Welds had a live-in maid, a competent forty-year-old spinster named Gussie who had been with them for six years, but it was her day off and she had left early that morning to visit family in Fort Lee, New Jersey. On reflection, Mrs. Berlinder told the detectives that she may have heard someone going out the back door as she came in the front. There was a service elevator in the back, usually run by the janitor, but he had not run it up to the fourth floor at all that day. Someone could have snuck down the back stairs and out the service entrance to the building, but he would have to have gone by the janitor's office and neither the janitor nor his helper had seen anyone. All of this was established within hours of the police arriving at the scene.

This made front-page headlines in the Friday morning papers, excepting only the *Times*, the *Law Journal*, and the *Daily Racing Form*, and the afternoon papers managed that rarest of all things for an afternoon paper, a scoop, when it was learned that Dr. Weld, who was not a medical doctor but a Ph.D. clinical psychologist, had been found in a "Manhattan Love-nest" with his "curvaceous twenty-two-year-old secretary," Lilly Latour.

On the third day after the murders interest fastened on Dossie McLamb, the maid in the apartment next door, who had been there alone while her employers were at work. She had had words with Mrs. Weld a few days before over garbage and who should put it where. But she was finally able to clear herself by showing that she had snuck away from her post and was at a studio across town taking a dance lesson at the time—she had plans to better herself by auditioning for a downtown burlesque show.

For a week or so after the murders the police made a public show of suspecting just about everyone who had been on the West Side above Fifty-Ninth Street that day. They questioned doormen, elevator men, janitors, delivery boys, bums—excuse me, homeless gentlemen—from the Hooverville in Central Park a few blocks away, everyone they could find who had been in the Seventy-Second Street Automat around lunchtime, and everyone who had been in or might have been in any of the forty-two apartments in the building. All of this was followed eagerly by every New Yorker who could read, and the sales of the major daily papers went up considerably, except of course for the *Times,* which had mentioned the crime in a two-paragraph story in the City Section on page thirty-two on the day after it happened, and ignored it thereafter.

* * * *

The investigators soon settled down to the operating theory that a person or persons unknown (read "Dr. Weld") had gained access to the basement storage area, climbed the back stairs and, using a key, entered the Weld apartment through the back door (now who would have a key to the Welds' back door?).

Finally last Tuesday in a major anticlimax, the police followed Dr. Weld to Grand Central Station, where they arrested him and charged him with the murder of his wife and son as well as Unlawful Flight to Avoid Prosecution. There was no direct evidence against him, and he was, by all accounts, on good terms with his wife and loved his son. But, after all, he had a mistress. He was therefore Beneath Contempt, as his murdered wife was Above Reproach. It was his misfortune that his mistress was also his secretary, so her swearing that he had been in his office all morning before they retired to their love nest in the afternoon was not as airtight an alibi as it could have been.

The *World* assigned a reporter and a photographer to the story, and they went all out. They bribed the building superintendent at 10 East Eighty-Fifth Street, where Dr. Weld had his ground-floor offices, to let Jerry Seindman, the photographer, in to take pictures. While he was there, Alan Shine, the reporter, joined him, and they rummaged through Dr. Weld's files for a list of his patients.

The "love nest," a one-bedroom apartment on Eightieth between Park and Madison, was harder to get to since the police had sealed the door and placed a guard at the downstairs door. Shine went over to the next building, one where you have to ring a bell to be buzzed in by a tenant. He rang several bells until one answered. "Hi," he said. "I'm a reporter for the *New York World*, and I'd like to interview you about Dr. Weld and his love nest. Did you know that it was right next door?" This got him and Jerry into the apartment and, about half an hour later, up to the roof. They crossed over to the love nest building, went downstairs, broke the seal on the apartment door and went in, which is where they were caught a half hour later by two detectives who had come up to conduct a second, or possibly third, search. When the cops opened the door they found Shine in possession of a pair of frilly pink unmentionables and matching bra. The conversation that ensued between the cops and the journalists is not beyond all conjecture. The *World* published the sensational scoop with pictures of the love nest and a description of the frilly undergarments, but without the photo. "They just didn't do it in black and white," the city editor explained to Brass.

Which prompted Brass to write a column about the Boundaries of Decency and where the line was that a newspaper should not cross. It was not, Brass explained, that there was anything wrong with frilly underthings or obtaining surreptitious entry to a place the police would bar you from to get a story. What he questioned was whether they should be telling *this* story in the manner they were telling it. He wrote:

> The power of the press is unbeatable for influencing public opinion and molding the readers' views on events both major and minor. This is why dictatorships like Hitler's Germany and Mussolini's Italy seize control of the Press as soon as possible after taking power.

Those of us who have access to such influence should use it judiciously in matters both small and large. Just as we should not urge our readers to tell Congress to close the borders against Chinamen or Mexicans merely because we do not happen to like Chinamen or Mexicans, or to buy a few additional battleships if one of our golf buddies should happen to manufacture the steel to make battleships, so we should not publish stories inciting our readers to prejudge the defendant in a murder case merely in order to sell more newspapers. By our own Constitution, which we profess to hold sacred, he is innocent until proven guilty to the satisfaction of a jury of his peers, whether he has one mistress or ten and whatever the color of her undergarments.

Well!

Sanders didn't even wait to call Brass up to his office, he stormed down to ours. "Chinamen?" he yelled, bursting through the door to Brass's inner office before Gloria or I could even slow him up, "I don't have anything against Chinamen!"

Brass looked up from his desk. "I didn't say…"

"Mexicans?" Sanders thumped his fist on the desk. "I don't give a damn about Mexicans!"

"Nowhere in the column did I even hint…"

"And just because I play golf with Ronald Patterson doesn't mean that I have some kind of damned interior motive about building battleships!"

"Ulterior," Brass said.

"What?"

"You don't have an ulterior motive."

"I know I don't, goddamn it. We need more battleships. We have to have a two-ocean navy."

"I thought we had a two-ocean navy," Brass said.

"They have to go around the Horn, did you know that?"

"Who does?"

"The battleships. They're too big to go through the Canal, so they have to go around the Horn if they want to get from the Atlantic to the Pacific. Or conversely."

"Why are we talking about this?"

"The *World* is writing stories about Weld because the murders were horrible, the story is sensational, and Weld is guilty as hell," Sanders stormed, "and, goddam it, it does sell papers, and what's wrong with that? And I don't want any of my staff saying or writing anything different!"

"I'm not on your staff, I'm a syndicated columnist. And I believe Weld is innocent," Brass said mildly—well, comparatively mildly.

"You *what?*"

Brass leaned back in his swivel chair and smiled up at Sanders. "I don't think he did it."

Sanders turned red and steam came out of his ears. You may not believe me, but I was there and I saw what I saw. "Out!" he yelled. He pointed toward the door. "Out! *Out!*"

And so here we were at nine thirty on a Wednesday morning in March, a good hour earlier than usual, setting up shop in Brass's living room. Garrett, Brass's man of all work, and I had just finished pushing furniture around, with an octagonal poker table as a desk for Gloria, and a comparatively easy chair in front of a glass-top coffee table for me. The sofa and a couple more easy chairs were gathered as though grouped for a still-life by the door. Brass was off two doors down the hall in his study, which, automobile books and magazines, stamp collection and other *objets de hobby* safely shelved, was now his office. I was just finishing sorting the day's mail, brought over from the *World's* mailroom through the falling snow and the slush of New York streets by Gertrude, one of the paper's runners, an apt job description, who was patiently waiting, hopping from foot to foot to foot, to see if I had anything to send back, when Brass appeared in the door a coffee mug in one hand and a copy of the morning's *World* in the other.

"Well, boys and girls," Brass said, "it's time to begin."

Gertrude stopped hopping and turned to Brass, her feet firmly on the floor in a perfect dancer's V. "Mr. Brass," she said. "I just want you to know, Mr. Brass, that the city room is five square behind you. That's what Mr. Hecht, the City Editor, said. Five square."

"Good to know, thank you," Brass said. "So you don't think Weld is guilty either?"

"Oh no, it's not that," Gertrude said. "We all think he's guilty. It's about Mr. Sanders firing you for writing what you thought, about fairness and the Constitution and that. Of course if any of us said what you said we'd be fired, not just kicked out of the office. But with you being syndicated and all—he could refuse to print your column if he wanted, but he'd be cutting off his wallet to spite his middle finger, is what Mr. Hecht says. I'm not exactly sure what it means, but I think it's smutty. Anyway, we're all rooting for you."

"Good to know," Brass said.

"So, do you really think he's innocent? Dr. Weld, I mean?"

"Your guess is as good as mine," Brass told her. "But I intend to find out."

"Good on you, Mr. Brass," she said. "Well I guess I should go." She turned to me. "Should I go?"

"It looks like we won't have anything for you," I said. "See you tomorrow."

"Right." She reached into her oversized canvas courier bag for a tiny coin purse, fished around inside it with two fingers, and triumphantly pulled out a nickel. "Ready for the bus," she said, and turned and skipped to the door. "Goodbye all!"

"Like that?" Brass asked, indicating her skimpy jacket with a wave of his finger.

Gertrude looked puzzled. "Like what, Mr. Brass?"

"You're going out into the snow like that?" he asked. "No overcoat?"

She shrugged. "It's not real cold, and I'm used to it."

Brass fished in his pocket for a silver dollar—he was fond of silver dollars and always had a couple with him—and tossed it to her. "Here," he said, "take a cab."

Gertrude considered for a second and then shrugged again. "Thanks," she said. "You're real," and skipped out the door.

"Well?" I said.

Brass turned to look at me. "Well?"

"It's time to begin," I reminded him.

"Then go," he told me. "Do so."

"I am merely your flunky," I told him. "It is for you to direct. So—in what direction shall I go?"

He raised his eyebrows. I think he practices that in front of a mirror. "Flunky?"

"Yes. It means…"

"I know what it means," he said.

"I am your flunky," I reiterated, "Gloria is your amanuensis and Garrett is your factotum. We each have our place."

Brass sighed a long-suffering sigh. "There is probably a place for you, Morgan," he told me. The doorbell rang before he could elaborate.

The doormen and elevator men have instructions to let anybody up who looks respectable and most of those who don't, without bothering to call first. Some of Brass's best sources are those who are not really sure they want to talk, and might be discouraged by an officious doorman.

Garrett went to answer the door, and returned with a skinny, very respectable-looking guy with a dark blue overcoat, a carefully-rolled black umbrella, a brown leather briefcase, and a black homburg. The man allowed Garret to take the umbrella, the overcoat and the homburg, but he clung onto the briefcase. The suit under the overcoat was a slightly lighter shade of blue. His face was oblong, his hair was brown, his ears stuck out a bit, and his nose was a bit large for his face.

He took a few tentative steps into the room. "Mr. Brass?"

Brass nodded. "Yes, sir. What can I do for you?"

"My name is Parcher. Mendel Parcher. I am an attorney."

"I conceal my astonishment," Brass said. "What can I do for you, Attorney Parcher?"

"I, ah, would like to speak to you. About Dr. Weld. Doctor Steven Weld. He is the—"

"I know who he is," Brass said.

"Yes. Yes of course you do."

"And you are his lawyer?"

"I have that, ah, distinction," Parcher told him. "May I speak with you? About his case?"

Brass waved him to a seat on the couch. "Speak away," he said.

"In, ah, private," Parcher said, perching gingerly on the front edge of the couch cushion.

Brass settled into the chair opposite and set his coffee mug and the copy of the *World* on the coffee table between them. "Miss Adams is my amanuensis and Mr. DeWitt is my, um, personal assistant," he told Parcher. "Letting them remain will save me the trouble of relaying what you say to them after you leave."

"Ah," Parcher said. He thought it over. "Are they your employees?" he asked after a minute. "That is, do you actually pay them a salary?"

"I do," Brass said. "Although why—"

"Here," Parcher said, reaching into his waistcoat pocket and pulling out a folded up dollar bill, which he unfolded and handed to Brass. "I am now hiring you, and by extension your employees, to consult with me in the matter of Dr. Steven Weld."

"Ah!" said Brass. "I see."

I didn't. While I wouldn't sneer at a dollar—it would, after all, buy a decent dinner for two at Pietro's if you didn't drink much—it wouldn't keep the Brass menage afloat for as long as it would take this guy to say what he had to say. And Brass valued his own independence too much to be hired by anyone. He didn't work for Sanders, as he had often explained to me during one of their disagreements, he sold him a product. And if Sanders ever became too disenchanted with the product, Brass would sell it to someone else. Which was why Sanders might kick Brass out of his office, but would never even threaten to stop running the column.

Parcher leaned forward. "Now, as my paid consultants," he explained, "you are covered by attorney-client privilege in regard to Dr. Weld."

Ah! Now I saw. Clever.

"I'm sorry to take up your time," Parcher said.

Brass smiled. "You're paying for it," he said. "Coffee?"

"No. No thank you."

"Then perhaps—"

"No, nothing, thank you."

"So. What can we do for you?"

"I'm not sure. Perhaps you'll have some suggestion. My client—Dr. Weld—is about to be put on trial for his life, and I believe he is innocent, as apparently do you, but that won't do me much good in court with the DA determined to prove him guilty." He rocked back on the cushion and then forward again, his eyes intently fixed on Brass. "By the way, what was it that caused you to believe that Dr. Weld is innocent?"

"Nothing you can use," Brass said. "What was it that convinces you?"

Parcher thought that over for a minute. "A confluence of several things," he said. "Steven is an old friend. We met in college—Princeton, class of '24. We were both Gamma Delta Iota."

"Gamma…"

"Stands for 'God Damned Independents,' what we called ourselves. Not members of any Greek club."

"Oh, yes," Brass said.

"Weld refused to join a fraternity on principle, although I have never been clear as to just what that principle was. I was not asked, probably because I'm Jewish. There is no Jewish fraternity at Princeton."

"And this formed a bond?"

"Yes, I think so. Some of us started Gamma Delt one evening when were in a local speak somewhat boozed up. It certainly seemed a good idea at the time. We actually went ahead with it, although it didn't seem quite so brilliant when were sober the next day."

"So you and Dr. Weld shared this non-fraternal bond?"

"That's about it. Then I went to law school at NYU and he got his Ph.D. in Psych at Yale, but we stayed friends. I respected him. He was—is—a real *mensch*."

I must have looked puzzled. Brass turned to me and explained. "It's Yiddish for 'man,' but it implies more, I think 'true gentleman' might cover it." He turned back to Parcher. "Is that about it?"

Parcher nodded. "Maybe even more, it means like a really honorable stand-up guy. Someone you can count on."

"Ah!" said Brass, filing the expanded definition away for later examination.

"I act as his lawyer for those few things that he needs a lawyer for," Parcher said. He paused and added, "And now this."

"You haven't really explained why you don't think he's guilty," Brass said.

"Right. Well, this is, ah, confidential…"

"Of course. You have my word. Our word," he added, with an enveloping sweep of his arm.

"Well, you see," Parcher thought for a moment, then plunged ahead, "he was planning on asking for a divorce."

An almost tangible silence settled over the room. Brass leaned back in his chair and stared at the ceiling, and then brought his gaze back down to the lawyer in front of him.

"A divorce? And this is why he didn't kill his wife? If the prosecution knows that, they'll be measuring Dr. Weld for the electric chair."

"Yes. Well. The District Attorney doesn't know and, I hope, won't find out. Steven had just started discussing the possibility with me. I know how it would look, which is why I can't use it. But, you see, he didn't want anything from the divorce—he was going to give her everything. Everything. The house—they have a house somewhere in the Hamptons—all the money, not that there is very much—everything. And pay alimony and child support, the whole ball of wax."

"Everything?"

"That's right. He said he still loved Helen. And he didn't want to hurt Billy."

"Then why—"

"He wouldn't discuss it. He just said he couldn't live with her anymore."

"That's it?" Brass asked. "That's why you think he's innocent?"

"That and because Debbie swears he really was with her."

"Debbie?"

"His secretary. Lilly Latour. Her real name is Debbie Wasserman. She's my niece."

"Your niece?"

"Yes. My sister's child. She wants to be an actress."

"An actress?"

"That's right. Hence the Lilly Latour."

Parcher had, unwittingly, just scored points with Brass. Anyone who used "hence," or "thus," or "consequently," or other terms of subtle erudition in normal conversation went up in Brass's estimation. Conversely, those who used words like "ascertain," or "emolument," or threw in phrases in French or Latin or, much worse, Greek, were definitely *de trop* and *mal de mer*, if I have that right.

"How long has she worked for Dr. Weld?" Brass asked.

"About, I believe, eight months."

"And how do you feel about their, ah, relationship?"

Parcher shook his head. "Their 'relationship' isn't what you think. But that's another part of the problem. How can you prove a negative?"

Brass leaned forward, looking interested. "In what way isn't the relationship what you think I think it is?"

Parcher spent a second sorting that out. "He would go to her apartment," he began, "but not for, um, an assignation. It began when they'd go over at lunchtime and she'd poach him a couple of eggs. Her apartment is only a few blocks from the office. He always closed the office from twelve to one thirty and it was that they'd both go to lunch, usually at the Schraffts on Seventy-Ninth. But when the Schraffts closed for repairs last month—water damage I think—she suggested that she make them lunch. He always has poached eggs, which is, as she puts it, no big deal."

"But you say there's no romantic interest?"

"I admit I asked her," Parcher said. "Because, you know, it did seem… But she says no."

"Just poached eggs?"

"Just that. Nothing more, ah, personal. Sometimes after lunch, Debbie says, Steven would sit on the couch and, as she puts it, go away somewhere. He would stare into space and look very sad."

"Well. Did she ever ask him why?"

"She was, not exactly afraid, but unwilling to. It seemed so personal."

"Have you asked him why?"

"I haven't asked a thing about it." Parcher spread his hands wide, and then dropped them back in his lap. "I didn't want to know anything more than I already knew. I thought—you see, I am not a criminal lawyer. I thought I would be handing the case over to someone who knew what they were doing."

"And?"

"And as of now he can't afford it. His only real property, the house in the Hamptons, is heavily mortgaged; his practice brought in enough to live on but not really enough to get ahead. And, obviously, nothing is coming in now. His wife had a trust fund, but Mrs. Berlinder, his mother-in-law, is seeing that he can't touch any part of it."

"So he has no lawyer?"

"Well, he has me, I'm not going to quit on him. But, truthfully, I don't know what the hell I'm doing in a criminal case."

Brass was silent for a minute, then he picked up the copy of the *World* from the table and held it out to Parcher. "Have you seen today's paper?"

"No—no I haven't."

Brass unfolded the paper and handed it across the table. "Bottom left," he said.

Parcher took the paper, stared down at it, closed his eyes and shook his head, and looked down again. "*Merde*," he said, which I don't think is Yiddish. He crumpled the paper and let it fall from his hands.

I grabbed at the paper as it fell and smoothed it, turning to the offending corner of the front page.

CONFESSION IN WELD MURDER CASE
BY ALAN SHINE

In an exclusive interview with District Attorney Mallory this reporter has learned that the DA's office now has the sworn testimony of an unnamed informant claiming that, in a long private conversation he had with Dr. Steven Weld, the doctor confessed to the murder of his wife Helen and their son Billy. The confession included details known only to the police and to the killer. Dr. Weld, who is now awaiting trial for the two murders, is being held incommunicado by the police. His attorney, Mendel Parcher, could not be reached for comment. (cont. on p. 3)

"This is crap!" Parcher said. "Crap!"

Brass stood up. "Can you arrange for me to go see Weld?" he asked.

"Yes," Parcher said, "certainly. I think so."

"Good," Brass said.

"That," Parcher said, pointing a quavering finger at the paper in my hands, "is crap—utter and complete crap!"

"I believe you," Brass said.

"But who...why?"

"It's probably some police stoolie who wants to get out of some minor burglary or pickpocketing beef. They put him in a cell next to Weld and go away and—presto—two hours later Weld has, for some inexplicable reason, confessed all to this complete stranger. Or so he says. It's a standard prosecutor's tactic. In their defense, they usually only use it on people who they think are really, really guilty."

"That's...that's..." Parcher stuttered.

"Yes, it is," Brass agreed. "See if you can arrange to get me in to see Weld sometime in the near future. And, while you're at it, write a note to your niece telling her it's okay to talk to Mr. DeWitt here."

"Ah, all right. Tell you what, I'll call her, tell her to expect him. Tell her he's on our side."

"Good idea," Brass said. "And, with your permission, I'll see what I can do about getting Weld a decent defense lawyer. Although, with luck, we can end this before we have to go to trial."

"Then you really do think he is innocent?" Parcher asked. "And you'll help?"

"Yes, and yes," Brass told him.

"I can't pay you..." Parcher began.

Brass made a patting gesture in the air with his hand. "I wouldn't let you if you could," he said. "I'm even going to give you your dollar back. But don't worry—your confidences will be honored. It would be unethical for journalists to take money from someone they are or may be writing about."

Not that a lot of them don't do it, I thought. But I kept my mouth shut.

"Where's your phone?" Parcher asked, looking around vaguely. Gloria led him through into the hall, where Brass kept one of his two phones, the other sat on the desk in his study.

Before I left an hour later to see Miss Latour, I asked Brass if he really thought Weld was innocent, or was he just stringing the lawyer.

He paused in the act of tamping tobacco into his briar, a sign that he was planning to ponder something. When he had something to ponder he would smoke one of his pipes and stare out a convenient window. I think different pipes are selected for different sorts of pondering, but I haven't yet broken the code. "What do you think?" he asked.

I pondered. "Before, I would have given you ten to one that he was guilty," I said, "but now it's even money."

"Ah!" he said. "I'll take your bet. Better than that, I'll give you three to one that he's innocent."

"Why? I didn't hear anything that couldn't be twisted either for guilt or innocence depending on who's doing the twisting."

"A couple of things," Brass explained. "One was that he asked for a divorce."

It lay there for a second, and then I picked it up. "I thought you said that if the prosecution knew that they'd be measuring him for the chair."

"And so they would," he said. "But consider—whoever did this spent some time thinking it out, you agree?"

"I do?" I asked.

"Certainly. Our unknown had to get to the back stairs, either through the lobby or through the service door in the rear of the building, without the doorman or the janitor noticing, which requires a certain amount of fore-knowledge, and he had to have a key to the back door of the Weld's apart-ment. He then had to let himself in without alerting Mrs. Weld or the child."

"Perhaps he was a friend or relative," I suggested.

"Quite possibly he was," Brass agreed, "but coming in through the back door would have required a bit of explanation. Our unknown then killed two people without any fuss, without even trying to make it look like a rob-bery, and faded away as quickly and quietly as he came. I'd say it was well planned."

"And Dr. Weld didn't do it because?"

"Because if he'd planned it that carefully, why on earth would he have told his lawyer that he was thinking of getting a divorce? It would take the arrow of suspicion, which was going to be pointed at him anyway, and turn it into a spear."

"Hmm," I said.

"And he wouldn't have spent the afternoon with his secretary, even— especially—if she was just poaching him eggs. He would have known what people would think."

"Hmm," I said.

* * * *

Which is why I found myself going up an elevator to the eighth floor at 132 Central Park West about two hours later. Lilly Latour, *nee* Debbie Wasserman was staying with her Uncle Mendel for the indefinite future. She couldn't—just couldn't—go back to her own apartment where the police and reporters had been upsetting furniture and pawing through her underthings.

She was waiting for me at the door to the apartment. A short, slender brunette with a face worth looking at and a body that might well be, but at the moment was wrapped in an oversized white terrycloth bathrobe, she looked younger than her twenty-two years and more innocent than a puppy. "Mr. Dewitt?" She stepped aside to let me walk past her. "My uncle said I should talk to you."

"If you don't mind," I said.

"About Steven? Dr. Weld?"

I waited while she closed the door and let her lead the way. "That's right."

"It's horrible what's happening to him," she said. "Of course it's even more horrible what happened to his wife. How could anyone do a thing like that? Here, let's go into the living room."

We went through a pair of glossy white-painted wood-framed glass doors, held open by two identical brass cats about ten inches high, and into a beige living room with green trim. Debbie saw me looking at the cats and said, "That's Bast."

"Excuse me?"

"Bast. The Egyptian cat god. Uncle Mendel likes Egyptian stuff. But he hates cats. Funny." She settled into an armchair of some fuzzy almost-white fabric and tucked her legs under her, pulling the bathrobe tight. I sat on the couch opposite. "I can give you about half an hour today," she said, "then I have to finish dressing. I have an audition in Brooklyn at six, and I want to get there early."

"Brooklyn? Really?"

"Don't be surprised. There's a lot of theater in Brooklyn."

"I know," I told her. "The Eldert Players, the Buzz Art Group, the Flat-bush Theater Guild."

She was impressed. Few people in Manhattan ever go to Brooklyn, hence they know nothing of the theatrical delights that await them just across the bridge. "My friend Peter Shay—you know, the director—set for me to read for this part," she told me. "*Green Grow the Lilacs*. It's a revival."

"I saw it on Broadway a few years back," I told her.

"What did you think?" she asked. I knew what she was asking.

"I think there are a couple of parts for you in it," I told her.

She smiled. "I haven't read the script yet," she told me. "That's why I want to get there early, so I have time to read the script."

"Good thinking," I said.

"Yes," she said. "Now, I really want to help Dr. Weld, but I don't know what else I can do. Like I told the police, he really was with me that day. He didn't leave the office until we went to my apartment for lunch, and he just sat there on the couch after lunch. He had no patients after lunch and he just didn't feel like going back. He did that sometimes. Staring across the room at the wall, but looking like he was seeing through the wall to the other side if you know what I mean. And he was still there when the police called at about four thirty."

"They called him at your apartment?"

"Yes. We have an answering service and they know to route the call through to my place if it's important. So they did."

"So he was with you from—what—nine in the morning to four thirty in the afternoon when the police called? The whole time?"

"That's right. So there's no way he could have done that—you know—that…"

"I know," I told her, "and I believe you. But it's going to be a rough sell, what with you two being lovers and all…" I braced myself.

"What!" She jumped out of her chair. Then she sat back down. "I am—I'm not—I wouldn't—I know everybody thinks that…" I saw that she was crying, but I don't think she noticed; she was paying no attention to the little tears that were running down her face.

"It's okay," I told her. "I believe you. You wouldn't. Is it because he's—was—married?"

She shook her head. "I wouldn't because I wouldn't with anyone. I don't believe in—that. Not until we're married."

"Oh. Of course not," I agreed.

She gave me a look. "I know it's cool to, you know, just do it. But I couldn't. And certainly not with Dr. Weld."

"You don't like him?"

"I like him a lot. He's not just my boss, he's my friend. But, you know…"

"I do?"

"He's…*old!*" She said.

I think I would rather be tried for murder than be cleared by a beautiful young woman saying "he's…*old!*" in that particular tone of voice.

"But the police won't believe me," she went on. "This one detective—Dorkin, I think—kept yelling at me to tell the truth. He said I'll go to prison as an accessory if I keep lying. But I'm not lying."

"Of course you're not," I said. I leaned back and thought for a minute. Then I said, "We have to figure out who might have killed his wife if he didn't. Did you ever meet her?"

"One time. She came up to the office to give Dr. Weld something—I don't remember what. Dr. Weld introduced us and she said hello."

"That was it?"

"Yes. Just that once."

"Did he ever talk about her? Say anything about who her friends were or what she liked to do, or go, or anything?"

It was Debbie's turn to think. She scrunched up her lips, which twisted her nose and was very cute, but I tried not to think about that because I was on the verge of being, you know, old.

"I did overhear a conversation once," she said. "It was between Dr. Weld and a doctor named Bloom. They refer patients to each other." She trailed off.

"And?" I encouraged.

"It was about his wife. It was on the phone and I, ah, forgot to hang up my extension."

"Of course," I said. "Very natural."

She looked at me suspiciously. I tried for a bland, neutral expression. After a moment she went on: "I was going to hang it up—I was! But then I heard Dr Bloom say, 'You know I can't tell you that.' And I was still going to hang up, but Dr. Weld said, 'All I want to know is, is she cheating on me or not? I'm not asking for specifics.'

"'You can't get much more specific than that,' Dr. Bloom said. And so I listened. I mean, I couldn't not."

"What did they say?" I asked.

"I feel funny talking about this," she said.

"Good," I said. "And if it were for any other reason than getting Dr. Weld out of the deep trouble he is in, I wouldn't ask you to."

She nodded. "Okay. You're right. This time. And I shouldn't have listened, but I did, and wouldn't it be strange if this helps him. Okay." She took a breath. "So what he said, Dr. Bloom, I mean, is, 'Are you sure you want to know?' and Dr Weld says, 'I have to know, 'cause I think she's lying, that she's not really having an affair, and I can't figure out why she would say that she is.'

"And Dr. Bloom says, 'I don't think she's lying exactly. But I don't think she's telling the truth either. I can't really go any further than that.'

"And Dr. Weld says, 'What does that even mean?'

"And Dr. Bloom says, 'I can't go any further, I really can't. You know that. But I think she still loves you, and I think you can work it out. And please don't ask me any more.' And he hangs up. And so I quickly disconnect, and that's what I know."

"Well, it's something," I said. "But not lying and yet not telling the truth—you have any notion what he meant by that?"

She shook her head. "Not a clue."

"He never said anything…"

"No, not ever."

"Okay," I said.

"That would sound dreadful if I told the police," she said, "so I'm not going to. I mean, he really didn't do it, and it would be horrible if they believe me on one thing and not the other."

"You're right," I assured her. "But there might be something in it. Which Dr. Bloom is he?"

"Harold, I think. It's in the card file on my desk in the office."

"Okay," I said.

"Do you think that it might help?" she asked.

"I have no idea," I told her.

* * * *

At six that evening, while Lilly Latour was presumably braving the wilds of Brooklyn, I was back at the apartment, in Brass's study, which was now his office, reporting on my visit. "Did you believe her?" he asked when I was done.

I nodded. "I'll give you ten to one he's innocent," I told him. "I believe she's telling the truth, but I'm damned if I see how we can prove it."

"What convinced you?"

"One line," I told him. "And I quote: 'He's…*old!*'"

Brass sighed. "The innocent cruelty of youth," he said. "We're set to see Dr. Weld tomorrow morning at nine thirty, that is if you'd like to join me."

"You didn't see him this afternoon?"

"He was getting a psychological evaluation this afternoon, at the behest of the DA."

I grinned. "They're giving a psychologist a psych evaluation?"

Brass nodded. "It's not as silly as it sounds if you assume he's guilty. It's so he can't claim he was crazy when he killed his wife. The prosecution can't lose however it turns out. If their psychologist finds him sane, then he's sane. If he finds him crazy, then he's a cold-blooded conniving killer who knows how to fake out another psychologist."

The doorbell rang.

A minute later Garrett escorted a well-dressed middle-aged woman into the office. She was every inch the suburban matron, from her black cloche hat and matching elbow-length black gloves to her black low-heeled shoes with the oversized bows, and the fur stole draped precisely over her shoulders. She stomped into the office, anger radiating off her in almost visible waves. "Mrs. Berlinder," Garrett announced.

She looked from the one to the other of us and settled on my boss. "Are you Brass?" she demanded, stopping in front of the desk and glaring down at him. "Are you the man who says my bastard of a son-in-law did not murder my daughter…"

"Madam," Brass began.

"…and my grandson?" she finished.

Garrett closed the office door, but I noticed that he stayed inside—in case we needed help subduing an angry woman, I suppose.

"I did not say Dr. Weld was innocent," Brass told her.

"Well, you implied it!"

"What I wrote was that it is not the job of a newspaper to decide on the guilt or innocence of anyone. That is for a jury of his peers."

"And they will find him guilty!" she declared. "And I'll watch while they hang him."

"Electrocute," Brass said.

"How's that?" she asked suspiciously.

"Electrocute. We electrocute people in New York. We have a special chair just for that."

She plopped down in the chair opposite him across the desk and glared at him for a minute, and then said, "Are you trying to be funny?"

"It's the furthest thing from my mind," he assured her. "What makes you so sure that Dr. Weld killed your daughter? There isn't any direct evidence against him."

"He mistreated her," Mrs. Berlinder said. "She told me. He seemed so kind and considerate on the outside, but inwardly—She couldn't take it anymore. It was him—he drove her to—she was thinking of leaving him. She told me."

Brass stared at her for a moment, thinking, and then he asked. "Just what did he do? What sort of thing? Did she tell you?"

"It was emotional," she said. "Emotional. He would make her cry. He would accuse her of things—horrible things. She told me."

"Did she tell anyone else? Complain to the authorities? Speak to a doctor?"

"Some things you only tell your mother," Mrs. Berlinder said, nodding her head up and down in affirmation. "She would call me when he went out, crying over the phone. But she wouldn't tell me just what he'd done. But a mother knows."

"Did he threaten her?"

"He must have, mustn't he? And he flaunted his affair with that—that—floozy."

"The lady claims there was no affair," Brass said mildly.

"Well she would, wouldn't she? It's women like her...she...she..." Mrs. Berlinder lost all words and was reduced to making inarticulate noises for about thirty seconds, then she suddenly stood up, turned, and marched out of the room. Garrett followed her out.

Brass stood and went over to the window behind him, his hands clasped behind his back. "It has stopped snowing," he commented. "Central Park has been whitewashed by the falling snow. Look—you can just see the carousel circling in forlorn splendor, the snow unbroken for yards around."

I went over to look. So it had. That sort of observation stuck into one of his columns is why Brass has a duplex apartment on Fifth Avenue and I am his flunky. I might have managed, on looking down at the park spreading beneath the window, "Gee, look—snow."

"Did you pick up anything from what Mrs. Berlinder said?" he asked.

"Yes," I told him. "She's pissed."

"There was a hint," he said, "perhaps—never mind, I'll think on it over-night. See you tomorrow morning."

"What time?" I asked.

"Oh, around nine will do."

* * * *

I was awake and out of bed at six the next morning, which is the sort of thing that happens when you have no social life and get to bed by ten. My usual morning occupation was to spend two hours sitting at my Remington writing the next great American novel. And so I sat. I wrote three pages. I crumpled them up and tossed them. I wrote a new page. I stared at it. It did not burst into flame, and neither did it dissolve into a pile of goo. It was time to leave, I had to meet Brass for our trip to wherever they were keeping Dr. Weld. I would let the page age in the typewriter. I took a cab to Brass's apartment. It was only twelve blocks, but hell, what's thirty five cents to a sport like me?

Brass was waiting outside for me and jumped into the cab. "Centre Street," he told the driver. "240 Centre Street."

"They're keeping him at police headquarters?" I asked.

"I think they've moved him down there especially for us," he said.

"Why...?" I asked.

"They have rooms there with very thin walls and people listening on the other side. And I believe these days they've gone up-to-the-minute, with hidden microphones in the tables and a stenographer at the other end."

"I thought the cops weren't supposed to listen in on a suspect's conversation with his attorney," I said.

"They're not," he agreed. "Nonetheless..."

When we arrived we were led into a ten-by-ten room with two doors, a battered metal table in the middle, and a large mirror on the far wall. There were three chairs on our side of the table and one on the other. Mendel Parcher was sitting in one of the chairs on our side. We nodded our greeting and went over and sat in the other two.

In about three minutes two cops brought Dr. Weld through the other door, took his handcuffs off, and sat him in the facing chair. Then one of them murmured "fifteen minutes" and they retreated and closed the door behind them.

Weld tried moving the chair around before discovering it was bolted to the floor, frowned, and then looked up at us and grinned a strained and tired grin. "Hi, Del," he said. "What brings you here? Who are your friends?"

Parcher made the appropriate introductions.

Weld nodded. "A pleasure to meet you." he said, shaking hands across the table. "Well, not exactly, but you know what I mean, the circumstances being what they are." He made an inclusive gesture around him. "Excuse the decor. Sorry I can't offer you anything to drink. I know I could sure use a drink."

"We'll work on that," Brass said.

"Del says you think you can get me out of here," Weld said.

"With your help," Brass told him. "Before we begin, here, look at this." He handed Weld a folded slip of paper.

"Okay," Weld said. He took it and read it silently and then handed it back and nodded. I took it from Brass's hand and looked at it.

THEY ARE PROBABLY LISTENING. DO NOT MENTION DIVORCE. IF I SHAKE MY HEAD STOP TALKING ABOUT WHATEVER YOU'RE TALKING ABOUT.

I stuffed it deep into my pocket.

"Since we believe that you didn't kill your wife," Brass began, "we need to figure out who did."

Weld shook his head. "I can't help you there," he said. "I've been trying to figure that out since the day it happened, and there's just nobody. She had no enemies, there was nothing worth killing for in the house, and...and..." He dropped his head into his arms, which were resting on the tabletop.

"Well, if she had no enemies, who were her friends?" Brass asked.

Weld raised his head and stared into space. "You know," he said, "it's odd. I don't know if she was close to anyone anymore. I mean aside from our mutual friends like Del here and his wife. She's been very, I don't know, closed in. She seems—seemed—to have dropped away from her women friends. Particularly since the miscarriage."

"Miscarriage?" Parcher asked. "I didn't know."

"No," Weld said. "Nobody knew. Only her doctor. And, I suppose, her mother. It was about two years ago. We didn't even know she was pregnant until she was six, maybe seven, weeks along. Then two weeks later it was over. She, well, neither of us wanted to talk about it. She didn't even want to talk to me about it. Then she went on this crazy kick…"

He paused, then shrugged. "I guess it doesn't matter now."

"What?" Brass asked.

"Helen—well she developed this fixation a few months after the miscarriage. She said the child hadn't been mine, and she should just leave me and she was so ashamed. I tried to talk her out of it but…"

"Did she say whose child she thought it was?"

"She refused to tell me, obviously because there *was* no one else. I'm not claiming that if she was having an affair I could instantly tell, but it didn't make any sense."

"How's that?"

"Well, for one thing, she was afraid of getting pregnant—I mean even before the miscarriage. She thought that somehow she was responsible for Billy's heart condition. The doctors told her that it wasn't hereditary, that it was just one of those things that happens in every, what?, ten thousand births for no known reason. But she said that no known reason meant it could have been her. She had an uncle who died of a heart attack. But for Christ sake, he was sixty-seven."

"So that…" Brass began.

"Also it made her compulsive about taking care of Billy," Weld went on. "I don't think she would have let him out of her sight long enough for her to have an affair."

Brass took out the reporter's notebook he always carried—I guess it made him feel more like he worked for a living—and wrote something, then turned it around and pushed it toward Weld. I leaned over to read it. *WAS THE DIVORCE HER IDEA?*

Weld looked at Brass and then sighed and nodded as Brass put the notebook back in his pocket. "Yes," he said. "Yes, it was."

Let the listeners make of that what they would.

Brass stood up and extended his hand across the table. "Thank you for meeting with us, Doctor," he said.

Parcher half rose to his feet, and then sat back down. "That's it?" he asked.

"For now." He shook Weld's hand.

"But…" Parcher said as Brass knocked on the door behind us to be let out.

"We'll be in touch," Brass told him.

"Thank you," Dr. Weld said.

"For what?" Parcher demanded as we were let out the door.

I waited until we were walking down Centre Street. "Well?" I asked.

"Well what?" Brass kept walking. He liked to walk. We were probably going to walk all the way back up to Sixty-Third Street.

"Well, are we any closer to catching the real killer?"

"Yes, I think so."

"You think she actually had a lover?" I asked. "I can see why Weld wouldn't want to admit that, even to himself. How do we find the guy?"

Brass didn't answer for five blocks. Then he said, "I think we have one chance to clear this, and it may not work. But we have to try."

"Okay," I agreed. "What do we do?"

* * * *

At ten fifteen the next morning Mrs. Lucy Berlinder stalked into Brass's living room two steps ahead of Garrett, purse clutched firmly in her hand, eyes glaring. "I almost missed the train," she said. "What is this news you have for me?"

"Let's go into my office," Brass said, and he got up and escorted her down the hall. Alan Shine, the reporter who was covering the case, was sitting in a chair in the corner as we went in. I knew that, since I had let him into the apartment for a private talk with Brass about half an hour earlier, but why he was there, or for that matter why Mrs. Berlinder had been asked to come in from Valhalla this morning, I had no idea. Brass does not like to burden me with unnecessary information.

"Sit," Brass said, indicating the chair that she had jumped out of the day before. He went around and settled into his desk chair. "Let me introduce," he began, indicating Shine in his corner chair, "Inspector Cramer of the New York City Police Department, Homicide Squad."

My mouth may have opened, but I quickly closed it.

"A pleasure, Mrs. Berlinder," Shine said, nodding. I noticed that he had retrieved his overcoat and his fedora and was now wearing them. It gave him an air of officious importance and impatience that went well with being a police inspector. "We'd like to thank you for your assistance."

She glared at Shine, and then turned the glare back to Brass. "What's this about?" she demanded.

"We do have to thank you, Mrs. Berlinder," Brass told her. "Without your alertness we might not have caught the real killer."

"Yeah," Cramer/Shine affirmed, "that's what gave us the clue. That's why we followed it up."

"The real...?"

"That's right," Brass said. "You see, your son-in-law was on the phone at the exact time you heard someone leaving through the back door. So it couldn't have been him."

"That's nonsense!" Mrs. Berlinder started out of her chair.

"No it isn't," Brass said. "Not at all. Telephone company records have confirmed it. There's no way he could have been the one who killed his wife—your daughter."

She sat back down. "But I…"

"So we started double-checking everyone's alibis," Shine said, slapping his hand emphatically on the side of the chair. "And what do ya know?"

Mrs. Berlinder seemed to shrink a little in her chair. "What?" she asked.

"That girl—that Dossie McLamb," Shine said, shaking his fist dramatically, "she was lying about where she was at."

"She's the maid who works in the next apartment," Brass volunteered.

"Yes, yes, I remember," Mrs. Berlinder said.

"Well, we has got her," Shine said. "She wasn't taking no dancing lesson—she was back in the apartment—your daughter's apartment. She was robbing stuff, and we figure as how your daughter caught her at it. So she grabbed up a knife and cut her throat."

I noticed that becoming a police inspector had played havoc with Shine's elocution, but I kept my trap shut. What were they playing at?

"Are you sure she…I mean…" Mrs. Berlinder began.

"There's no doubt about it," Brass said. "I mean *somebody* killed your daughter, and it wasn't Dr. Weld. And she had a bracelet that we figure must have belonged to Mrs. Weld. We're going to ask you to identify it."

"Yup, that's right," Shine said. "We got her cold. And she's going to fry. They'll sit her in the hot squat and pour the juice through her." He paused and looked thoughtful. "You know," he said, "I think you can smell the kind-of singed smell when they turn the current on."

Mrs. Berlinder was definitely shrinking into her chair now, and she looked sick.

"And it's your testimony that's going to guarantee her conviction," Brass said, leaning forward.

"Yeah," Shine said, getting up and taking two steps toward her. He leaned over. "With your help, we're going to put her in the hot seat. I guarantee it!"

Mrs. Berlinder collapsed in the chair and put her head on the desk and started crying. "I can't," she said in a cross between a choke and a squeak. "I just can't."

"She is going to be convicted," Brass said. "That's certain!"

"Oh you men," Mrs. Berlinder cried, "you're all so smart!"

"Why, what do you mean?" Brass asked.

"Don't you want to see your daughter's killer convicted?" Shine demanded.

"She didn't…didn't…do it!" Mrs. Berlinder cried, pushing herself up to a sitting position with both palms cushioning her face. "She didn't! Oh, it's horrible!"

"She didn't what, Mrs. Berlinder?" Brass asked, leaning in even closer until his face was only inches from hers.

"Come on, she must have!" Shine insisted loudly. "Who else could have? Don't worry, we'll see she gets what's coming to her."

"I never thought," Mrs. Berlinder cried. "I mean, I thought…I mean… Oh dear God!"

"What is it, madam?" Brass demanded. "What are you trying to say?"

She took two very deep breaths, holding each one for a few seconds, and then stood up. "I can't," she said.

"If you have something to tell us," Brass told her, "then you must speak."

Another deep breath. "That girl," she said. "Dossie. She didn't do it."

"She must have," Brass said.

"She'll be convicted," Shine added.

Mrs. Berlinder stared wildly around the room like a trapped bird, and then collapsed back down in her chair. "My daughter did it!" she cried. "Helen killed herself!"

For a while, I'm not sure how long, there was no sound in the room except Mrs. Berlinder crying. Brass leaned back in his chair and Shine retreated to his corner. Then Brass said, "I'm sorry, Mrs. Berlinder. I'm so sorry. I can't imagine how painful this is for you."

"Yes," she said.

"There was a note?"

"Yes." She fished in her purse for a long time and then passed over a well folded piece of paper.

Brass unfolded it and read it. He didn't pass it to me then, but later I got to see it. It read simply:

I can't go on. It's better this way. I'm sorry. Helen.

"And the knife?" Brass asked.

"It was next to her. I took it away in my handbag."

Brass nodded. "Because if there was no knife then it couldn't be suicide."

Mrs. Berlinder stared at him for a long moment. "Yes," she said finally. "And then the blame would go where it belongs—to her husband. He drove her to it. And killing Billy—my grandson—he must have…he must have…"

"I think not, Mrs. Berlinder," Brass said. "I think—I think that spiritually your daughter fell down a well and couldn't see any way to get back up."

"I don't know what you mean," she said.

"It's not an easy thing to accept," Brass told her. "It happens sometimes to some people and we don't know why. And they do their best to hide it from the rest of us so we don't know how much help they need. Perhaps the miscarriage, coming after Billy's heart condition, was just too much."

She began crying again.

"Why don't you rest for a while," Brass said. "Morgan will show you to our guest bedroom. Lie down. If you want anything—coffee or tea or any-thing—we'll bring it to you."

She allowed herself to be led out of the room. As we reached the door, she turned. "Scotch," she said. "Scotch and water."

I showed her to the guest bedroom and then brought her a large Scotch and water. "If you want anything else," I said.

"I think I'll lie down," she said.

* * * *

When I got back to the office Brass was just getting off the phone with the real Inspector Cramer. "Okay," I said, "How did you know?"

"I wasn't sure it would work," he said, "But it seemed the best shot—maybe the only one. Assuming there was a note, she took it and the knife away with her to make it look like murder. But I didn't think she could live with someone other than her son-in-law being blamed. I was betting on her being an essentially decent woman."

"Not that," I said. "How did you know it was suicide?"

"Oh that." He shrugged. "Well, we knew that Dr. Weld didn't do it. That 'He's *old*' convinced me. What is it that Sherlock Holmes says? 'When you eliminate the impossible, whatever remains, however improbable, must be the truth.' Something like that."

"It was the knife!" Shine volunteered from his corner seat.

"That was one of the pointers," Brass agreed.

I looked puzzled.

"Consider," Brass said. "You've just murdered a woman in her apart-ment. Now you want to get out of there and as far away from the scene as possible. So you take the bloody knife with you? Why not just wipe off the fingerprints, drop it on the floor, and go? On the other hand, if you want to remove any chance that it may be thought a suicide, and you haven't had time to think it out, you take the knife away with you."

"What the mother should have done," Shine added, "was drop it in the kitchen sink."

"What she should have done was leave it where it was," Brass said. "But she thought Dr. Weld was truly responsible for her daughter's suicide, so why not get him blamed for it."

"Anything else?"

Brass thought for a second. "Some of what she said when she came here to yell at me suggested that she might be suppressing saying something else. But I was listening for it, and perhaps I was mistaken. I had to break her down. It was not fun."

"Speaking of which," I said. "I think you owe the maid—Dossie McLamb—something for turning her into a murderess, even if she doesn't know about it."

Brass considered. "You're right," he said. "I'll call Minsky, he can always use another dancer."

The author of more than forty published books, **Michael Kurland** lives on California's central coast with his partner, novelist Linda [L.F.] Robertson, a dog, a cat, two raccoons, several opossums, various representatives of the suborder Sauria, and two dozen fruit trees. His latest novel, *Whatever the Cost*, is a sequel to the espionage thriller *The Bells of Hell*. Reach him at michaelkurland.com.

A FIGHTER BY HIS TRADE

GRAHAM POWELL

Even way down under Madison Square Garden you heard the cheer from the ring. Mr. Nicholas the masseur looked up and grinned. "Gotta be a knockout, hey, Charley? They don't cheer like that for nothing else."

"Sure sounds like it," I said. He rubbed a big bruise on my side and I winced.

Nicholas smiled again. "Feels like you took some hefty shots tonight."

"He got me pretty good all right, but I didn't go down."

"When was the last time you was on the canvas?"

I thought it over. "Maybe '60? '61? I'm not too sure anymore, but it's been a while."

He started working on my arms and shoulders and I guess I drifted off. Next thing I knew, there was some kind of commotion out in the hall. The attendant came in and said, "There's some people here—" but before he could even finish, this big swarthy guy in a suit pushed through with three or four others in tow. I saw one of them was a woman and I blushed, 'cause all I had on was a towel.

The big guy beamed at me and said, "There's the kid I want to see! You were great up there tonight, really terrific. I've never seen anybody take shots like that before."

"I can sure take a shot," I said. "I haven't been down since '61."

"That's what I like," he said. "A tough guy, takes his lumps and keeps on coming, a guy who never quits. Wasn't it you who took Albert Salerno to ten rounds?"

I thought about it. "Yeah," I said. "I think maybe I fought that guy seven or eight years ago. Went the distance but lost on points."

The guy laughed. "My name's John Massey," he said. "You've got a chance to be a great fighter. How'd you like to come work for me?"

"Oh, you better talk to Mr. Fletcher about that. He's my manager."

"That's what I'm telling you, son! I just bought your contract." He turned and shouted, "Fletcher, get over here!"

Mr. Fletcher came in from the hallway, wearing the nice gray suit he always wore when I fought at the Garden. His face looked a little gray, too. "Hey, Charley," he said. "That was some fight tonight."

"Thanks, Mr. Fletcher. Is it true what he's saying, that you won't be my manager anymore?"

"Yeah, Charley, it's true. I'm getting old, my health isn't as good as it once was. Managers have to be tough, too, Charley, to get guys like you the fights they deserve. Mr. Massey can do that. He'll stick up for you. Me, I can't do that like I used to."

"Are you still gonna come see me?"

"I wouldn't miss it, Charley." He smiled. "Keep your chin tucked in. I'll see you around."

He shuffled out the door. I felt like I should say something but then he was gone.

"It's not his fault, Charley," said Mr. Massey. "If you haven't got your health, what have you got?"

Somebody laughed. Massey said, "Hey, you must be starving. I know a place with the best steaks in town."

"Okay," I said. "But I'm really not dressed for it."

They all laughed at that.

* * * *

I showered and got into my street clothes, and we took a big limo over to a place in Brooklyn. They seemed to know Mr. Massey there—we walked right in past a line of people waiting.

They put us at a long table in the back. The woman who was with them sat next to me. She wasn't much more than a girl, really, with brown hair cut short, brown eyes, and bushy brown eyebrows. She smiled and offered her hand. "I'm Clara."

"Hi, I'm Charley Robertson. Are you Mr. Massey's daughter?"

She laughed. "I'm not that young! No, I'm his office girl."

"Oh, so you work for him. I guess I work for him too now. So we're uh, co-leggs?"

"Colleagues," she said. "That's right. You're not from New York, are you Charley?"

"No, I grew up in Altoona. I didn't come here until after I got out of the army. If you want to be a boxer, New York is the place to be."

"I'm from… It sounds like a joke but it's not. I'm from a town out on Long Island. It's called Hicksville."

I didn't mean to laugh at her, but I couldn't help it. "A New Yorker from Hicksville! I never heard of that!"

"I got out of there as soon as I could, believe me. I've lived in Manhattan for six or seven years now." She glanced around and leaned closer. "Charley, why did you say you'd fought Albert Salerno? You couldn't have fought him."

I frowned. "Maybe I got his name wrong? It was a long time ago."

"Albert Salerno is *John's* real name."

"Oh yeah?" I said. "He doesn't look like a fighter."

"No, Charley." She sighed. "It was a test. He was testing you."

"Well, I'm sure glad I passed."

Then they brought out the steaks, and we all dug in.

Massey had to leave the table to take a phone call, and when he came back he was beaming. He raised his wine glass. "A toast!" he said. "To Charley Robertson, my new favorite fighter, who has a date with Jericho Bailey in six weeks!"

"Wow," I said, "Bailey's a good fighter. Am I gonna be sparring with him or something?"

"No, kid, you're gonna be in the ring! I talked to some guys and we all agreed that you two ought to fight."

"But he's a middleweight. To go up against that guy I'd need to pack on like ten pounds."

Massey laughed. "Then you'd better have another steak."

Later on, when I was helping Clara into her coat, Mr. Massey came over and spoke to us. "You two getting along all right?"

"Yes sir, Mr. Massey," I said.

Clara smiled and said, "Charley's a prince, John."

"Well, good, because you're going to be spending a lot of time together. Charley, I called Walt Skinner up in Poughkeepsie and you're going up there to train with him. I rented an old farmhouse just outside of town. Clara, you go along and keep this mug company. Don't let him get into any trouble." He winked. "*Any* trouble."

* * * *

Mr. Skinner was a good trainer. I'd fought some of his guys before. They were always ready and didn't make too many mistakes. You went up against one of his fighters, you knew you were in for a long night.

First day, six miles of roadwork down old country lanes, a five-pound weight in each fist. I was plenty sore when I got back but Mr. Skinner just barked, "Get your lazy ass in the ring, pug!" So I had to go fifteen minutes, and not five rounds, either—fifteen minutes straight with no breaks, with two guys taking turns against me. I puked after ten minutes and Mr. Skinner just mopped it up and told me to keep going.

When I could eat, Clara made lunch—six eggs and a steak. I still didn't feel so hot but I kept it all down. "We gotta put as much meat on you as we can," said Skinner. "Otherwise this Bailey kid will beat you silly." Then he had me on the speed bag and the heavy bag for another hour.

When I got back to the farmhouse I could barely get up the steps to the front porch. Clara had fixed meatloaf and, I told her it was pretty good.

"Thanks." She put her hands on her hips. "You know, I'm not really here to cook."

"Aw, don't say that. You're a really good cook," I said.

"I suppose. Do you want to do... anything else?"

"I like to play gin rummy."

We played gin rummy.

Mr. Massey came down at lunchtime in the third week. Clara brought him back to the kitchen, where I'd just finished eating and was sort of slumped over the table. "How are you doing, Charley? Skinner keeping you busy?"

"I think Mr. Skinner doesn't like me," I said. "He's sure putting me through it."

"All in a good cause, son. When you go up against Bailey you'll thank me."

He turned to Clara. "You enjoying playing house?"

She shrugged. "I won twenty-five bucks off him at rummy."

Massey laughed. "I see you're a man of iron constitution, Charley. I'm looking forward to seeing it in the ring."

That sure made me feel good.

*　*　*　*

"Remember," said Mr. Skinner. "This kid does everything well but nothing great. You're great at taking a punch. Just stay on your feet and you'll do fine."

The fight was on a Thursday at the Sunnyside Garden Arena in Queens. It wasn't Madison Square but it wasn't bad. I'd been on the undercard one night when Floyd Patterson fought there. Jericho Bailey was a black kid too, from somewhere down in Virginia. He was tall for a middleweight, with long arms, and he sure had some muscle on him. Now I knew why Mr. Skinner had me eating all that steak.

Mr. Massey was there at ringside, with Clara sitting next to him. She sure looked nice. The referee explained the rules, then the bell rang and we went at it.

In just a few minutes I could see what Mr. Skinner meant. Bailey could land his punches all right, but he didn't have as much power as he maybe should've. I got in some good shots of my own and heard him grunt and curse. Though he was bigger than me I could lean on him and keep him against the ropes, where he couldn't use those long arms to jab at me.

After seven rounds of that I guess he got mad because he really started coming after me. He caught me flush on the temple and I staggered a bit, and I guess he thought I was hurt because he came wading in. But he couldn't get me down and after a while he punched himself out.

I was afraid I was behind on points but Mr. Skinner just kept saying,

"Stay on your feet and you'll be fine," so I didn't try to press too much. After the bell to end the twelfth we stood together in the middle of the ring while they read out the scores. Turned out two of the judges had it seven rounds to five, and the other called it dead even. I'd won.

Bailey wasn't happy about it. "Man, that's bullshit!" he said, loud enough for all the fans to hear. "I beat on this cracker all night, and you say *he* won? Fuck all you!"

His manager grabbed him and said, "Shut up, Jerry, shut up and you'll get another chance!" Finally they headed off to their locker room.

Later on we went out to a place that Mr. Massey knew down in Little Italy. They had a small room in the back and we all crowded in there. Mr. Massey seemed really happy, laughing and waving his cigar around. He even gave the waiters each a couple of cigars.

"Charley, you gotta come out to my place on Long Island sometime," he said. "It's right on the ocean. You like fishing? I got a boat, rods and reels, all that crap. You come out and we'll make a day of it."

"Thanks Mr. Massey. I'd like that."

Someone said, "Make sure he don't fall out of the boat, Johnny!" and they all laughed.

"Fishing ain't as dangerous as it used to be," said Mr. Massey, chuckling. "Back then a lotta guys fell out, am I right? Much safer these days."

Clara said, "How'd you get to be fighter, Charley?"

"Let me think," I said. "I started boxing when I went in the army in '52. I didn't go to Korea, they sent me to Germany instead. I was a lightweight back then. I got out, I guess it was a couple years later. There weren't a lot of fights out in Altoona so I moved up here. I fought Tony DeMarco in '56, and Kid Paret in '60. So I guess it's been what, ten or twelve years now?"

Suddenly Clara wasn't smiling. "Charley," she said, "It's 1969."

"Oh, yeah? Time sure flies, huh?"

* * * *

That was in April. My next fight was at the end of July.

"Now this guy Rooney," said Mr. Skinner. "He's not like Bailey. *This* guy can put you on your ass. So you're gonna have to be careful out there, you can't just soak up punches."

"Yes sir, Mr. Skinner."

We were watching a film of Danny Rooney beating up some poor Mexican kid. "Rooney's got a weakness," Skinner said. "He tips his uppercut. Watch right here—see how he drops his right? That means he's loading up to throw it. As soon as you see him drop that hand, you come over it with a left hook. Got it?"

"Yes sir, Mr. Skinner."

"Good, kid." He smiled. "Let's go work on it."

We stayed in New York this time, and I worked out at Skinner's gym down on Delancy. He'd got a couple guys about Rooney's size for me to spar with, and showed them what he wanted. I must have thrown a hundred hooks a day. After a week I was seeing Rooney in my dreams. Twice I woke up thrashing around in the bed, my hands balled into fists.

Clara wasn't cooking for me this time around, but she'd still come around at lunch and dinner so I wouldn't have to eat all by myself. Sometimes we'd play a little rummy. I must've gotten better at it because I won back all the money I lost in Poughkeepsie.

The fight was back in Madison Square garden, but not the main arena—it was in a smaller hall called the Felt Forum. Me versus Rooney was the main event. The last time I did that was, well, it must have been six or eight years ago at least.

Clara and Mr. Massey were there right by the ring. She waved at me when I came down from the dressing rooms. There was a pretty good crowd, too. I guess most of them were there to see Rooney; I think every second guy had red hair.

"Remember to look for that right hand, kid," said Skinner. "Don't mix it up with this guy, don't take too many big shots. Just stay on your feet."

The bell rang and Rooney practically ran across the ring. I covered up and let him wear himself out on my arms and shoulders, then I started chopping away at his guts. He kept trying to push me off, to get some room to really wind up, but I stayed on him.

After a few rounds of this he was getting tired and frustrated, taking more chances and leaving openings. I got in a couple nice shots, even busted his lip. After that *he* was the one covering up, *he* was eating punches, and I was giving him all he wanted. I got in one nice shot to the ribs and Rooney grunted and danced away. I went after him–

—then suddenly I was looking up at the ref standing over me.

"Three! Four! Five!"

"Get the fuck up, Charley!" shouted Mr. Skinner. "Get your ass up right now!"

The canvas stank of sweat. Getting up felt like crawling up a mountain but somehow I made it. Before Rooney could come at me again the bell sounded.

I staggered back to my corner and just about fell onto the stool. "I told you not to mix it up with this guy!" said Mr. Skinner. "Now we have to fight his fight!"

Suddenly Mr. Massey was there by the ring. "You goddamn imbecile," he said. "You're gonna fuck up everything! You gotta get this guy on the ground, do you hear me? Get this guy on the fucking ground, or else!"

"Yes sir, Mr. Massey," I said.

I was still pretty wobbly so I turtled up the next round and let Rooney do what he wanted. I didn't give him a good shot at my head but he made up for it with what he did to my ribs. When the round was over I could barely move.

"This is it, kid," said Skinner. "Final round. You have to knock him down. You can still win it, but you *have* to knock him down. Got it?"

I was too tired to do more than nod.

We went out and touched gloves. Rooney stayed back and made me come after him. All the roadwork I'd done paid off then. My legs were heavy but they kept going as I tried to trap Rooney. I could see he was tired but he wasn't no quitter.

Just as he slipped under a right and dodged away I hear Mr. Massey shout, "Did you come here for a fight or a footrace?" That got the biggest cheer of the night, and I could see Rooney's face get redder than it was already.

He came in and gave me a couple of pops before fading back again.

Clara yelled, "If you want to dance I'll be your partner!" and the crowd roared again.

Rooney was mad now, really mad, and came straight at me, throwing haymakers. I dipped and dodged, landed when I could, and kept my eyes open.

"Don't you know when you're beat?" he said.

"Show me, you bastard," I said.

He stepped in and dropped his right.

I didn't even realize I'd thrown a punch until I felt the shock up my arm like a jolt of electricity. Rooney stumbled back and tried to catch himself on the ropes, missed, and went down on his knees. Knockdown.

I looked over at Mr. Massey and he was on his feet, with Clara cheering and clapping beside him.

Rooney was up by the count of eight. We danced around for another thirty seconds, but I didn't want to take a chance and neither did he. After the bell it took the judges a few minutes to add up the scorecards. The ring announcer looked them over and said, "Ladies and gentlemen, the winner, by unanimous decision—Charley the Rock Robertson!"

The place went bananas, people cheering and jumping around. Mr. Massey howled like a wild Indian, Clara jumped around like she was possessed, and Rooney even came over and shook my hand.

I had to yell to be heard. "I'm sorry I called you a bastard!" I said.

"That's all right!" he shouted. "I'll take it out of your hide in the rematch!"

* * * *

But there wasn't gonna be a rematch.

The next morning Mr. Massey sent his car around to pick me up and take me to his office. It was pretty swank, all shiny wood and leather and brass. He was having breakfast when I got there. "Want some steak and eggs, Charley?" he said.

"I think I've had enough steak for a while, Mr. Massey," I said.

He laughed. "Not for too long," he said, and tossed a newspaper onto the table in front of me.

It was open to the sports pages, and my picture was right there at the top, under the headline "Old Dog Learns New Trick."

"They love you, kid," said Mr. Massey. "Listen to this: 'Veteran pugilist Charley Robertson last night hit the canvas for the first time in eight years, but got up to win both the fight and a new nickname: Charley the Rock. His defeat of local favorite Daniel Rooney has earned him a date with defending champion William Sligo...' You hear that, Charley? You're the number one contender!"

"Me, Mr. Massey?"

"You're damned right! Later this morning we're going downtown to sign the contract. You're fighting for the title!"

So they found me a suit to wear and we all went down to City Hall. There were a bunch of reporters and they took pictures of me and Sligo signing the contract in the big hall, then we went out front on the steps and they took more pictures while we pretended to fight.

Once it was all done Sligo came over and said, "Charley, you probably don't remember me, but when I first moved to New York you sparred with me a few times."

"Yeah, sure," I said. "I think I remember that. What did you say your name was?"

"It's Little Billy Sligo. That's on account of my uncle Big Billy. He was a heavyweight." He stuck out a hand and we shook. "I sure am glad it's you I'm going up against," he said. "Couldn't happen to a nicer guy."

After he'd gone Clara came up and leaned against me. "While we're here we could get a marriage license."

"Oh," I said. "Uh, well..."

She laughed and then I knew she was joking. "Come on," she said. "You can walk me back to my place."

So we walked uptown in the afternoon sun, me in my new suit and her in her best dress, and things seemed pretty good. I think I could've just strolled around like that for the rest of my life. That would've been just fine with me.

"Charley," she said after a while, "have you gone out with any women since you came to New York?"

"Just whores," I said. "Not any nice girls."

She stopped and laid a hand on my arm. "Look at me, Charley. What do you think *I* am?"

"I think you're a real nice lady," I said. "Not like them whores."

We walked on until we got to her building. When she said goodbye, I saw that she was crying. I didn't know how I'd hurt her feelings but I sure felt bad about it.

* * * *

Though the fight wasn't until December, I trained with Mr. Skinner five times a week. Every day he was bringing in different guys with different styles. "Sligo can fight any style, so you gotta be ready," he said. It was just like back when I learned to fight at Fort Dix.

Clara came over a couple times a week and we'd have lunch or dinner. We went to a movie once. It was called *Midnight Cowboy* but there weren't any Indians or even horses and it took place in New York.

I won ten dollars at rummy but now I figured she was letting me win.

Later that week, Mr. Massey had me come to his office. He was on the phone when I got there but waved me into chair. "Charley's here," he said. "I'm looking at him right now. We sure found the right guy, huh? Did you hear the latest odds? Now it's down to three-to-two. Sure, it's short money but it's a sure thing. This fight will get a lot more attention, so we gotta be careful. Let's talk it over at dinner. Lombardi's at eight, right."

He hung up and smiled. "Sorry about that, just some business. Guess who's coming up here today?"

"I don't know, Mr. Massey."

"Ever hear of W.C. Heinz?"

"Is he the ketchup guy?"

Massey cracked up. "You say the funniest things, kid. No, this guy is a sportswriter. He's going to write a story about you for the *Saturday Evening Post*. Everyone in America is going to know your name."

"What's the story going to be about?" I said. "I mean, I never really done anything. I went in the Army, I learned to fight..." I shrugged. "And here I am."

"You'd be surprised the things these writers can get out of you, things you didn't even know yourself. And hell, he wrote a novel about a boxer. If he has to he can make it all up."

Clara came in then with a stack of papers for him. "Hey, Charley," she said. "Ready for your interview?"

"I sure hope so," I said. "I hope I don't say anything stupid. So you're the office girl here?"

Mr. Massey nodded. "I couldn't get along without her," he said. "The women in my life keep me organized. At home I have my wife, and here— here I have Clara."

He gave a real toothy smile that made me feel kinda funny, but maybe I was just nervous.

* * * *

I'd never fought the main event at Madison Square Garden before. Sure, I'd been on the undercard plenty of times, fighting four or six rounds, but this was fifteen rounds for the world championship.

As we waited for them to call us out, Mr. Skinner said, "You just do what old Fletcher told you to do, Charley. Keep that chin tucked in and you'll be okay."

When I walked out, everybody in the place was on their feet, clapping and cheering. I hurried down to the ring. All the attention made me nervous.

Little Billy Sligo didn't look nervous. He smiled and waved at everyone, even waved at me. I started to wave back and then thought maybe I shouldn't.

We met at the center of the ring. The referee said, "I want a clean fight. Break when I tell you with no bullshit. Defend yourselves at all times. Now go to your corners and come out fighting."

The bell rang and the fight was on.

Billy came out dancing, circling to his left, flicking his jab. I stayed buttoned up and didn't chase him, just waited for him to come to me. He'd swoop in and get me on the jaw or over the ear a couple times and then slide away, but I kept after him. He was looking for a chance to land a bomb, and we both knew if he got that chance then it would be over.

In the fourth he got me pretty good over the right eye. Blood started pouring out and I couldn't see too good, but when the ref asked if I wanted to continue I said yeah. After that Sligo kept working on the cut and it got worse and worse.

In the sixth he landed a right that I didn't see coming and put me on my ass. I got up somehow and stayed up until the bell. "Whaddya think?" said Mr. Skinner. "You ready to call it a day?"

"I can still fight!" I said.

"You'd better, or I'm throwing in the goddamn towel."

I'd never quit a fight in my life and I wasn't about to start now. I knew I had to do something so I started chasing Billy around the ring, firing lefts and rights as soon as he was in reach. I was wearing myself out but it didn't matter—if I couldn't catch up with him I was done for anyway.

After the bell to end the eighth I didn't sit down, just stood in my corner while they cleaned me up. If I sat down I wasn't sure I could get up again. I wasn't going to make it another seven rounds. One way or another it would be over soon.

We met in the center of the ring. "What are you doing, Charley?" he said.

"Come get some, Little Billy," I said.

So we stood in the middle of the ring trading punches like a couple of schoolkids on the playground. I wish I could say I got the better of him but that's not true. Sure, I got my licks in, but he beat the hell out of me. A shot to the gut folded me over and a right to the cheek put me down.

I hadn't gone down since '61 and now I'd been on the deck three times in my last two fights. I looked out towards the crowd with my face pressed to the canvas… and there she was.

Clara was in the front row. She must have been standing on her chair. Even with all the noise I know I heard her shout, "Come on, Charley! Get up! Get up!"

And I did. Billy was standing over in the neutral corner and he looked surprised to see me on my feet. Once the ref finished counting, Billy came over and poked at me kind of gingerly, like he was afraid he'd hurt me.

"You'll have to do better than that," I said. I launched a shot to his ribs.

He flinched and took a step back but I stayed on top of him. I got him again, then twice more, and then he was back in the corner, covering up. It was like I'd gone crazy—I worked my fists until my arms ached. He slid away against the ropes but I didn't let him get away, working right-left-right-left until the ref grabbed me and the bell rang and the fight was over. I'd won.

I'd won.

I'd won!

I looked over towards my corner. Mr. Skinner looked as stunned as I felt. I found Mr. Massey's face in the crowd. His mouth was hanging open in shock.

I don't remember much after that. They brought out the championship belt and strapped it on. Little Billy was finally able to get up and he came over and shook my hand. I stood there for what seemed like hours, listening to the people cheering.

Then I went back to the locker room and passed out in the shower.

* * * *

The following Friday I was sitting in Mr. Massey's office, smoking a big cigar. He had bags under his eyes. I asked, "Are you all right, John?"

"Sure, kid," he said. "Just real busy. You winning that fight took a lot of people by surprise, now everybody wants a piece of you."

"I'm a little surprised, too," I said.

He ran a hand over his face. "Listen, kid, right now you won't be able to walk down the street without getting mobbed. Why don't you get out of town for a few days? Me and some friends of mine are going out to my place on Long Island this afternoon. No one will bother you there. We'll drink some beer, shoot pool, maybe even go fishing. These people had a lot of money on the fight, and they're excited to meet you."

"Sure, John," I said. "I'd love to do that. Any friend of yours is a friend of mine. I'm just happy I can do something for you after all you've done for me."

"You're a good kid, Charley, and you've done more for me than I ever expected. I'll go call down and have them get the car ready. We'll stop by your place on the way to pick up some clothes."

While he was off doing that, his secretary stuck her head in the door. "Charley? Clara asked if you could come down to the file room, please."

She pointed it out and I went on down.

Clara seemed kind of down. "Hey, what's wrong?" I said. "You feeling okay?"

"Charley, I... there's something I need to tell you."

"Sure, you can tell me anything."

"I don't think you're going to like this. Charley, John and his friends, they bet against you last night."

"Naw, John wouldn't do that. Why would he do that? He's my manager."

"The last time Billy Sligo fought the odds were four to one. No one could make any money on him. So they built you up like you were a great fighter, and this time the odds were three to two. You heard John talk about it, 'short money but a sure thing', remember? They didn't think you could beat Sligo. You weren't supposed to win."

"I don't know what you're talking about," I said. "I never threw a fight in my life."

"You didn't have to, don't you see? They paid the judges in your other fights so as long as it went the distance, you'd get the decision. Why do you think they chose you? They needed someone who didn't get knocked out. And you hadn't been down in years."

"You can't talk that way about John. I wouldn't be where I am today without him. I owe him."

We stood there for a minute. I didn't know what else to say. When I turned to go, Clara said, "Wait, Charley. Why don't you and me go do something together? Have you seen *Hello, Dolly*? Or been out to the Bronx Zoo lately? Or we can go to Coney Island and ride the carousel, and maybe you can win me a prize. Then, later—if you want to—you can maybe come up and see my place."

"Well, gosh, Clara," I said. "I'd sure love to do that. But I promised John I'd go fishing with him. I sure hope we can do all that stuff another time."

"I hope so too, Charley," she said. She hugged me real tight.

John and me and a couple of other guys took the special elevator down to the garage and got in a big Cadillac. "I hope the fish are biting!" said one of them, and the other cackled.

John said, "Shut your yaps!" He turned to me. "Those guys don't know you like I do, Charley. I'll make sure this trip is easy as possible."

"Thanks, John," I said.

I felt bad for leaving Clara behind. She'd been crying when we said goodbye. I hated to let her down like that.

I hoped I got a chance to make it up to her.

Originally from Shreveport, Louisiana, **Graham Powell** has lived in his adopted city of Fort Worth for the last 15 years. His story "Pictures of Lily" previously appeared in *Black Cat Mystery Magazine*'s Private Eye issue. Other stories have appeared recently in the Anthony-nominated anthology *The Eyes of Texas* and in *Malice Domestic 16: Mystery Most Diabolical*. When not writing, he works as a systems engineer.

SMELLING LIKE A ROSE

GIL BREWER

Gil Brewer (1922–1983) was an American mystery novelist and short story author. Between 1951 and 1967, he published a stream of pulp paperbacks for Gold Medal and other companies, including such titles as Satan Is a Woman (1951), *The Vengeful Virgin* (1958), and *A Taste for Sin* (1961). He also found a ready home writing hardboiled stories for *Manhunt* and other mystery magazines. "Smelling Like a Rose" was originally published in *Mr. Magazine,* July 1957.

The tall young man arranged himself to better advantage in the yellow-and white-striped canvas beach chair beside the cabana, and went on reading the morning paper. The headlines were large and black and jarring:

MANIACAL KILLER SOUGHT
THIRD DISMEMBERED BODY RECOVERED

The young man read with nervous absorption, now and then glancing over toward a nearby pink stucco cottage, situated just above the creamy beach. Hot sun blasted the Florida landscape where tall royal palms stood listless beyond the smoothly sloping sands. It was early. Two bathers frolicked a quarter mile down the beach.

A woman with a strikingly lush shape, wearing a scant two-piece white swim-suit, lounged quietly from the front screen door of the pink stucco house. She was tall and ripe-looking, like a sun-shot plum. Her yellow hair was drenched with sunlight as she leaned against the jamb, holding the door open, staring across the twenty-five-yard space that separated her from the young man.

He read on.

"...body found ten miles from the first gruesome discovery. Doubtless all the work of the same killer, a strange fact has been disclosed by the police. All three victims were surrounded by a strong scent of roses. Several bruised petals have... "

The spring on the screen door whined.

The young man's gaze shot out to her. He threw the newspaper aside, lurched to his feet, husky, dark-haired, wearing khaki shorts.

They stared at each other. The woman's right hand lowered from her amply curved hip, and gently massaged the inside of her smooth bare thigh. Her eyes were opaque, her plump red lips faintly parted.

The young man formed the words with his mouth, smiling, but not speaking aloud. "Hello, there."

The woman's fingers squeezed her thigh.

A man's voice shouted from inside the pink stucco cottage. "Jean! Come on in here—you've let the damned eggs burn again. How the hell can a man expect—?"

She ran into the house. The screen door slammed.

The day was hot and still.

The young man hurried toward the white cabana, reached the patio, and went inside. Standing just beyond the closed door, in the modernistically furnished living room, he was breathing much too hard to blame it on the short walk from beach chair to house.

"Jesus," he swore softly. "Jesus Christ."

He stepped lithely over to the gold-upholstered studio couch, grabbed a heavy tan pillow and beat it with his fist. He held it in his left hand and smashed it brutally with his right. He hurled it from him. It plopped gently, with hardly any sound, against the wall and fell to the floor.

A man's curses roofed the morning. "I said, God damn you, Jean. How the hell much more do you expect me to take?"

The young man rushed to the large picture window on the side wall of the living room, sprawled across the studio couch, and peered over the sill at the pink stucco cottage. He was perspiring heavily. As he lay there, watching, he wiped himself dry with another pillow from the couch, his hands trembling.

"Oh, Jesus," he said. "Oh, dear, Jesus."

He said the words tightly against his front teeth with a kind of hissing. His strong brown fingers clutched at the pillow, tearing through into the sponge rubber cushion.

Somebody knocked on a rear door. The young man shot off the couch, turned half running, then stabilized himself. He stood perfectly still for a moment as the knocking continued, harsh, peremptory. He took long breaths, then walked through the hall into the bright yellow kitchen. There was a man at the door. The young man flung the door open.

"Here for the rent, Mr. Helman," the man said. He was a stocky man, in his early forties, wearing old white trousers, a T shirt, and he was badly in need of a shave. "That is," he went on, "if you intend to stay another week. You reckon you will?"

The young man started to reply, then paused.

Across the rear yards, the lushly shaped woman in the bathing suit was hanging clothes on a line. She leaned low over a wicker basket, her back to them.

"Mr. Helman?" the man said. He turned and saw the woman. He waggled his hand through the air and said, grinning, "Wow—Va-va-*voom!*" It sounded strangely ridiculous coming from him.

The woman turned and stared across the yards at them.

The young man snapped the words, "Yes. I'll be here another week. Just a sec."

He vanished into a room off the hall.

"That's eighty-five-fourteen," the man called from the doorway, his eyes on the woman.

The young man returned clutching some money. He thrust it into the other's hands, and said, "Keep the change."

"You like it here all right, Mr. Helman?"

"It's fine," the young man said, "perfect."

He closed the door in the man's face. Moving quickly, he went to the side kitchen window and watched the woman over there. The man who had collected the rent climbed into a pick-up truck, watching the woman, and drove off up the shell road toward the main beach highway.

She continued to hang her clothes, but fumbled often, because her gaze was on the young man's cabana.

The young man stood rigidly behind the curtains covering the kitchen window. He kept muttering unintelligibly to himself.

"Jean?"

The loud male voice called from the pink stucco house. The woman ran toward the house, then stopped, hands cupped under her breasts.

A tall, thin man, wearing rimless glasses stepped off the back porch and walked slowly across the yard to her. He wore a light gray suit, and the young man at the kitchen window seemed to strain himself, listening.

The man motioned toward a parked convertible under a carport, patted the woman's arm, then got into the car and drove away.

The woman watched him go, slowly turning until she was staring directly at the young man's cabana.

Helman moved fast, now. He hurried through the house and out the front door. He raced across the lawn just above the beach until he reached the other house.

She was already waiting behind the screen door.

"Hello," she said.

He stood in front of the door.

"You going to ask me in?" he said.

She rolled her full lower lip under her upper lip, then kneed the screen door open, and motioned him in with a toss of her head. She had amazingly thick blonde hair, flowing in rich wheaty waves around her shoulders.

She drew a long breath, watching him, and let it out with a slight shudder. They seemed to be static, locked in a current of their own making.

"My name's Vince," he said. "Vince Helman."

"Mine's Jean."

"We practically know each other," he said. "Don't we, Jean? We didn't really need the names."

"No."

She seemed unable to move at all, frozen, watching him, waiting.

His voice held a tight, hoarse tremor.

"Every day I watch you. You wash an awful lot of clothes."

"Yeah."

"I wasn't sure till today, Jean."

"You shouldn't have said that!" She turned, started walking away into the plushly furnished living room, then whirled toward him. Her buttocks humped under the taut white latex of the swim-suit, her thighs plumping out where the rims bit into her warm-looking flesh. "You shouldn't have come here. You know it."

He stepped toward her, a half step. "How in hell could I help myself?" he said slowly.

"He won't be gone long—Vince."

The place was very still now.

"He'll be back any minute. He's mad as hell at me." She talked suddenly, the words running pell-mell over themselves, stubbing their toes. "I wanted you to come," hoarsely, too, "I prayed you'd come over. I've been trying and trying to get him out of the house. All I can think about is what—it's like a—I can't help it!"

He reached her in one stride, took her in his arms, and they embraced passionately, his hands moving all over her body. She writhed against him, her red-nailed fingers digging sharply into his bare back, clutching at him. They mouthed each other, the woman moaning as if in actual pain.

"I'm mad," she gasped. "I'm damned near crazy!"

"I know—I know, I know."

"When you touched me under the water, swimming the other day, I nearly screamed."

He held her brutally, his hands tearing at the swim-suit. The latex stretched and tore, ripping without sound, and her flesh was released.

"No, Vince—not now. We've got to wait. Good God, if he ever caught us. He'll be back, I tell you."

"I've got to," the young man said. *"I've got to!"*

She fought hard, very strong, twisting, and broke free. She cringed away, and her flimsy bra fell to the floor with a soft splat, between them.

"That's why I wanted to see you now," she said rapidly. "It's our only chance—first one, anyway, before we work something out."

They were both breathing very hard.

She said, "He's going out tonight, Vince. He'll be gone hours. That's why I've been so careful. I've known ever since I saw you a week ago—how it would be. The way you look at me. It's been awful—he's my husband, but he's no good."

He took her in his arms again, kissing her. Abruptly, they broke apart as a car crunched to a stop in the carport. Immediately the engine was cut off, and a door slammed. Footsteps sounded on the rear porch.

"Watch for when he goes," she whispered. "Then come over to my bedroom. I'll be waiting, darling. Run!"

He ran. Her husband came in the rear. She rushed for the bedroom. Helman made it out the front screen door, closed it gently, and ran hard for the beach. He dove into the sand and lay there gasping, face down in the sand, taking the sun.

"Jean? Where the hell are you—oh. Shower?"

"Yeah. It took you long enough. You get everything?"

* * * *

Helman lay on the sand. The hot white sun beat down. The Gulf was like syrup. A broad V of pelicans thrashed along overhead, cumbersome, and somehow out of their element, even with wings.

After a time, Helman stood up and ran down and dove flatly into the water. He swam hard, churning, until he was just a flashing speck against the dazzle of silvery horizon. Finally, after floating for a time, he swam back and walked dripping slowly up toward the cabana, his eyes on the pink stucco house.

The afternoon waned.

Helman fixed some food from a can, put it on a plate and stared at it. He did not eat. He left it on the table, found a bottle of whiskey, poured himself a drink, but did not drink it. He flung open a drawer in the sink, brought out an icepick, and just then the telephone rang. He flung the icepick at the wall. It whipped off, bounced against the refrigerator and rattled violently spinning off across the floor.

He lifted the phone carefully.

"Darling—guess what I'm doing right now?" she said, breathing the words across the wire.

"What about—?"

"It's all right. He's in the shower, he can't hear. I'm lying on my bed, thinking about tonight, darling. Oh, honey, honey—it won't be long." Her voice was a passionate whisper, and Helman seemed to vibrate, standing there.

"Cut it out," he said hoarsely.

"I can't help it! Oh, honey—*honey...*" She hung up abruptly.

Helman slapped the phone on its cradle and paced the house. He stripped off his shorts and took an icy shower, then strapped himself dry with a rough towel. He seemed unable to stay away from the side windows of the house. In a few moments he was again covered with perspiration, talking to himself.

Night fell.

He did not turn on the lights inside the cabana at first. Then suddenly he leaped and turned his bedroom light on, and hurried back to the living room.

He watched the pink stucco house, white now in the moonlight. The Gulf washed quietly against the sands. Somewhere a gull screamed.

The convertible started loudly across the way. Helman was on his hands and knees on the studio couch. The car backed out and roared off up the shell road, headlights sweeping sear grass and palmetto.

The yellowed drawn blinds of her bedroom shadowed as she moved in front of the light, and Helman's breath was ragged.

He headed for his bedroom, slipped on khaki shorts, and hurried for the front door.

As he crossed the lawn, the pink stucco house looked very quiet, with only the bedroom light on, and he missed seeing the shadow of a pickup truck parked beyond his own house, in the trees. He stepped on the front porch, opened the screen door, and went in.

"Honey?" she called. "In here—in the bedroom."

Helman opened the bedroom door and stepped inside. Something smashed him brutally across the head. The woman quickly lowered a small, child's baseball bat, as he sank unconscious to the floor. Quickly, she handcuffed him, hands and feet, and already he was coming to.

He opened his eyes to her crooning face, saw her naked, perspiring body leering above him, and smelled roses. He saw the roses, banked against the walls of the room, like in a funeral parlor. He started to scream.

At that same instant, she plastered a broad strap of adhesive tape across his mouth. His eyes swelled as he stared at the gleaming knives arranged on the canvas tarp where she rolled him. He tried to scream, heaving, as she crooned on and on.

"Maybe you read the papers, my darling—I can't help myself. I have to find them like you—crazy, full of burning lust, half mad for something you'll never really have, like me."

She held a long knife poised over his chest now, her voice passionately crooning. "I've found a way, you see?—with roses like my father's grave, and my husband won't be back for days—we'll have so much fun together, because I love you," she said, driving the knife into his chest—"Love you!" she crooned excitedly, her plump red lips loose and wet. "Love you!"

Outside the bedroom window, the landlord, in white trousers, broke and ran stumbling off towards his pick-up truck, yelling hysterically for the police.